THE COACH
THAT NEVER
CAME

BY PATRICIA BEATTY

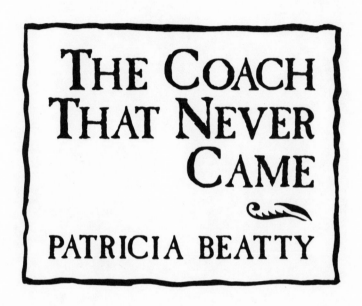

THE COACH THAT NEVER CAME

PATRICIA BEATTY

William Morrow and Company, Inc., New York

1 2 3 4 5 6 7 8 9 10

Library of Congress in Publication Data
Beatty, Patricia.   The coach that never came.
Summary: While spending the summer with his grandmother in Colorado, thirteen-year-old
Paul becomes involved in a dangerous adventure when he tries to trace the history of an unusual
gold and ruby belt buckle that his grandmother claims is a family heirloom.
[1. West (U.S.)—Fiction. 2. Colorado—Fiction.
PZ.B380544Co   1985   [Fic]   85-15213
ISBN 0-688-05477-3

BOOK DESIGN BY LAURIE GREEN

For my niece Michell Morgan's children:

Joshua

Wesla

Caitlin

and for their "Nana,"

Lorraine

CONTENTS

1

AN
HEIRLOOM
OF SORTS

One glance at his mother's face as she met him at the front door that last day of school gave Paul Braun the answer to the question that had burned in his mind all day long.

No.

His stepfather, Jesse, had called from halfway around the world, and she had received a reply from him—but not the one that Paul had been hoping for.

Kim Braun wasn't grinning with her usual welcome, though she asked cheerily enough, "How did the last day go? You aren't going to have to repeat the seventh grade, are you?"

Paul managed a laugh at his mother's attempt to be

funny, and told her, "There wasn't any doubt of that, was there? I've been getting A's and B's all along, so don't worry that I won't get into Phillips Academy in the fall." Then he added more seriously, "You talked to Jesse in Saudi Arabia and asked him about me, didn't you? He said no, right? I can tell from the look on your face."

Kim Braun let out a sigh. "Yes, I'm afraid he did. He called here an hour ago, and even though it was a bad phone connection, Jesse heard me when I asked about taking you to Europe with me for the summer next week."

"Why did he say no?"

"Because he wants to take a vacation with me alone; he wants us to go to Greece and Italy by ourselves. Please understand. We haven't seen each other for eighteen months, and I think he's planning some sort of second honeymoon. Paul, Jesse is good to you. He's going to send you through Amherst, his college, once you graduate from Phillips Academy. He's been a very good stepfather to you and a good husband to me."

Trying not to show the disappointment he felt, Paul turned away and walked into the big yellow kitchen. He took a can of soft drink from the refrigerator, and standing with it in his hand, he said, "Yeah, that's true. Jesse's been a better stepfather to me than my real father's been a father. I can see Jesse's point. I do understand. You and he have only been married for four years, and he's been away a lot of that time building bridges and power stations and palaces for oil sheiks. He's an engineer and has to go where his company sends him."

Kim Braun looked at her fair-haired, green-eyed son. Thirteen-year-old Paul resembled her in complexion, though he was going to be tall and lanky like his father, whom she had divorced when Paul was very small. His personality, though, was unlike hers or anyone else's in the family. He was old for his years. That could be because he'd been fatherless for so long and had been left with a long series of baby-sitters while she'd worked as a law secretary to support the two of them. Paul had never known his real father, who had simply walked out on the pair of them after a quarrel Kim had not thought important. He'd never sent her money for their son; and later she'd heard that, after the divorce, he'd gone to Canada, remarried, and fathered a family there. How happy she had been when she had met Jesse Braun, a most interesting, lively man, who had wanted both her and her son. He and Paul shared so many interests—stamp collecting, fishing, jazz, and history—that before long, Paul had taken to him. And Jesse had been wonderful to Paul, legally adopting him and giving him his name. Until Jesse's firm had sent him to the Arab emirate, the two of them had been like true father and son. Jesse had even agreed to send Paul to Phillips Academy, a private prep school.

Paul broke into Kim's train of thought, "Okay," he said, sighing. "You're off to Europe next week and I'll stay here in Wilmington. Do I go to camp all summer or does somebody come here to live in the house with me?"

Mrs. Braun smiled. "Neither." She took a deep breath and, still smiling, continued. "You're going out to my old stamping ground when I was your age—Colorado. You'll be spending the summer at your grandmother's house."

Paul set his soda down, then sat down himself. He muttered, "To grandmother's house I go—I go!"

"You'll like it. It's close to a hundred years old. Gothic with gingerbread all over—wait till you see it."

Paul's green eyes met his mother's. "Mom, sending me off to my *grandmother's* house sounds like kid stuff. Aren't I a little too old for that?"

Mrs. Braun said tartly, "No, I don't think so. You might even like Colorado. You saw a lot of your Grandmother Sally when she was last here over Christmas. You seemed to like her."

"Sure, she's a neat little old lady."

"Oh, she'd love to hear you say that about her!" More soberly Kim Braun said, "We haven't got much family, you and I. There's just you and me and her, Paul. I'm her only child since my brother, Lance, was killed in Vietnam before you were born. Then, when I married your father and came east with him it just about killed her."

"Grandmother could have come here to Delaware, too!"

"Paul, she loves Colorado. All her friends are there. Her side of the family has lived there for generations now."

"And finally I have to go visit the old homestead, huh?"

"Yes, you should, you know. Your grandmother's asked for you to come out for the summer last year and the year before, too. I called her just before you got home and told her you were coming to visit her. She came here to see you. It's your turn to go to her now. She was delighted to hear it."

"So you already told her?"

"Yes, I did. Don't frown so. You'll have a good summer."

"Did you tell her I wanted to go to Europe with you?"

A swift look of anger crossed Mrs. Braun's face. "No, I didn't! Why should I cast a shadow over her summer with you? Knowing that she's second choice would make her sad. I'm counting on you to go there and act as if you truly want to be with her. She deserves that! Jesse and I deserve some time together, too. It will be another year and a half before he comes back to the home office here and someone else is sent to Saudi Arabia in his place."

As Paul finished his drink, he turned his head away from his mother to look out the kitchen window. "Okay, you've made your points. I understand. I guess I'll get to Europe someday somehow."

"Of course you will. You'll go all over Europe—maybe backpacking on a college summer holiday the way Jesse did once."

"Uh-huh, maybe so." Paul sighed, then gave his mother

5

a smile that he didn't really feel. She was right. She did deserve some time alone with her husband.

During the next few days Paul packed for his summer while his mother packed for hers. He told his friends, who were chiefly bound for summer camps, where he was headed and noted their enthusiasm—even their envy. Would they be as jealous, he wondered, if they knew he'd wanted to go to Europe instead and was "settling" for number two, Colorado? He tried hard not to resent Jesse for leaving him out of their summer plans, and not to let his mother know his resentment. He hoped she wouldn't come back with some expensive present for him from Jesse. He didn't want any.

Paul and his mother left on the same day, flying from the same airport. His flight was first, so Kim saw him off with a kiss on the cheek and a bright smile. Just after his flight was called, she gave him a tiny little box, saying, "Give this to your grandmother, please. It's a gift for her for having you. It's a pair of peridot earrings. She loves green and they're her birthstone."

"Sure, I'll give 'em to her. Have fun in Europe." Paul shoved the box into his jacket pocket, hugged his mother, then hurried for the gate that led to the plane. How alone he felt. He'd flown before, but never by himself. Sitting in a window seat over a wing, he felt as though the whole world had turned its back on him. The elderly man sitting next to him dived into a financial magazine the minute the plane took off and even during lunch said little.

Because he was next to a wing, Paul saw little of the country he flew over. Colorado Springs Airport was not quite like others he'd seen. Jesse had once said that all airports were the same, but it seemed to Paul when he came into this one that the people were different. They thought he was, too. They stared at his well-pressed long blue trousers, loafer shoes, his pale blue oxford cloth shirt, and red-and-blue Madras jacket. They wore clothing that to his way of thinking was very casual—dark shirts and trousers.

And then he saw his grandmother. A little woman whose blonde hair was streaked with gray, she came rushing up to him and grabbed him in an embrace. She wore a brown gauze flounced dress and a turquoise and coral looped necklace. In Wilmington no one her age went around like that. With her deep tan she looked rather like an Indian to Paul.

"Paul, Paul, you're here at last!" She drew back from him and surveyed him from head to foot. He waited for her to tell him how he'd grown but she didn't. She simply smiled and said, "The first place we stop at on our way home's a clothing store. You look like you're in Cape Cod, not in Colorado. I'll bet you're all seersucker, designer jeans, polo and oxford cloth shirts in your luggage. We'll make you look Colorado in no time."

Paul stifled a groan. He said, "Grandmother, don't make me look like I just got out of a horse opera movie."

7

"No, no, no! We won't do that, but we will make you a bit less noticeable—a little less Ivy League." Sally Weber grinned. "Just wait till you see what I have at home for you as a welcome present."

"A horse?"

She laughed. "No, not a horse."

Humor her, Paul told himself. That was the thing to do. He changed the subject. "Mom gave me a gift to bring to you. I think it's to say thanks in advance for having me with you."

Again she laughed. "Aha, a bribe? Okay, come on now." She turned away and Paul followed her.

Once they had claimed his two pieces of luggage and left the airport in Mrs. Weber's old dark green car, Paul asked her, "How far is it to your house?"

"Six or seven miles from here. It's your house, too, remember? You'll inherit it someday—unless you want to give it to the city as a museum. They want it for that."

"Is it that old?"

"Yes, for this part of the country it is. The city has taken an interest in it." She turned her head as she drove to look at him. "It's not like some eastern houses that are two hundred years old and full of Revolutionary War and Civil War memories, but it's seen some history too since it was built in 1896. George Washington never slept there, but there's an old family story that Theodore Roosevelt did."

"Sure, I read about him. He was a president."

"Are you interested in history?"

"Sort of. Some of my friends don't like anything but today, but I like to read about old stuff."

"Your mother told me that you're a real reader."

"I guess I am. I read a lot."

"What do you read?"

"Science fiction, adventure stories, sports stories, mysteries, stories about interesting people's lives."

Again she looked at him and asked, "Paul, have you read much about the West?"

"Not much. I don't go for western stories. Mom turned me off them early, I guess, because she talks so much about the West. I think she used to be homesick before she met Jesse and married him. If she didn't have such a good job, I think she would have come back here with me to live."

"I wish she had come. Paul, there's a good branch library close to the house, and I have a lot of books, too. I'm something of a pack rat. I don't like to throw things away. I've kept some of your Uncle Lance's old books, too. You'll have his room. They're in it. You're welcome to borrow any of them. But you may want to go to the library, too, so you can meet some young people your own age. You might make some friends at the library."

Paul sighed inwardly. Who made friends at a place where all you ever heard was "Sh-h-h." It didn't seem to him that summer had started well at all. Where would he make friends here?

As if she had read his mind, Mrs. Weber said, "There's a video arcade not far from the house in the other direction.

It's full of boys and girls all the time. Do you like that sort of thing?"

"I got some games last year for Christmas, remember? They're all right for a while. Then they get boring."

"Well, I hope you find the gift I'm going to give you interesting. It belonged to your Uncle Lance at one time. He didn't take it when he went into the army. It wasn't a thing they would think highly of, so he left it home. I think it would be all right for you, though."

"What is it?"

Paul's grandmother laughed softly at his inquisitiveness. "You'll find out soon enough. Now, take a look at my town. It isn't much like Wilmington, is it?"

This certainly wasn't. Where Wilmington was flat and Colonial brick and cobblestones, Colorado Springs had Pike's Peak and other mountains to the west, north, and south; and on the east, prairie lands. And it was modern, all glass and steel, stone and wood. The streets were broad and paved with macadam. The air was clear and tangy. Paul was used to summer humidity, and the dryness and brightness here made his eyes ache so that he had to reach into his pocket for his sunglasses.

The dimness of the department store they entered was a welcome relief. Mrs. Weber led the way to the men's department, where she told a clerk, "My grandson here needs a windbreaker, three shirts, two pair of good, strong denim jeans, and the kind of shoes local boys his age wear."

Paul interjected, "Not cowboy boots, Grandmother."

10

"No, ordinary shoes to walk and run in."

"I play soccer," Paul told the clerk.

"Kids play that here, too. We can fix you up with some sports shoes and you'll be right in style."

"That's all right with me."

A half hour later, they left the store for the Weber house—the "homestead," as Paul had privately nicknamed it. When they pulled up in front, he could only stand and gawk at his first sight of it. It was a four-story house with balconies completely around the top three stories and a deep porch below. Painted glistening white, replete with scroll-work trim, it looked more like a wedding cake than a house. It stood alone, with wide green lawns between it and the other old houses nearby. So this was where his mother had grown up.

Mrs. Weber smiled at his gawking and said, "It's rather big for just me, isn't it? I rattle about in it. You can see why the city thinks it would make a good museum, can't you? Why don't you ask me the question everybody does?"

"What's that—how many rooms does it have?"

"No, that's the second question. The first one is—is it haunted? So far as I know it isn't. There are twenty rooms, big and small. Let's go in. I've got dinner in the oven. Your room's the first one on the left at the top of the main stairs. You'll know it by the red-and-white sign on the door that says 'Keep Out. Danger. Explosives.' "

"Huh?"

"Yes, Lance got that from somewhere and put it on the

11

door when he was your age. It was the fad then. I never took it down. Don't you kids do things like that now?"

"Not me or my friends, but I do have some big blowup posters of soccer games and people high-diving."

"That sounds colorful. I'll leave you alone for a while to unpack and put your things away in the closet and bureaus. When you're through with that, it should be time to come down and eat. You'll find the bathroom next door to your room." As she opened the front door, Mrs. Weber added, "Paul, why don't you put on some of your new clothes, too?"

"Why, is what I've got on now that bad?" Paul asked unhappily. "Are you expecting company for dinner?"

"No, no, no! It'll be just the two of us. After supper you'll see why I asked you to."

"Okay."

A glance inside the house showed Paul a central staircase with halls on each side of it and large open rooms to the left and right. The ceilings were high and the furniture was like props for a turn-of-the-century movie—big, heavy, yellow-colored wooden pieces with red velvet upholstery and fringes. He'd be spending the summer in a museum—not just walking through one but living in one!

Lance Weber's old room was a museum piece, too, but not like those he'd passed through below. It was out of a TV show about teenagers from the sixties. It had school pennants on the walls and photographs of boys with long, shaggy hair and girls in miniskirts, a plastic radio, and a single bed with a brown and red Indian blanket on it. It was sort of spooky being in somebody else's room, somebody who had died. Paul tried the radio but as he'd figured, it didn't work. No matter, he'd brought his transistor radio with him. He sighed as he flung a suitcase onto the bed. The room was weird looking, but this was where he was going to be sleeping for three months so he'd better get used to it.

Paul unpacked, putting everything away in closets and drawers. Then he changed into a pair of stiff new jeans, and a blue-and-yellow plaid shirt, and the new sneakers. Finally he picked up the leather belt his grandmother had picked out for him after rummaging through a whole rack of them before she was satisfied. He hated it. It was tooled leather with an intricate, flowing design on it. Frowning at his reflection in the mirror, he threaded it through the belt loops. He certainly looked different now. Well, he wasn't in a ten-gallon hat and cowboy boots, and that was something to be thankful for. Just the same, he'd be stared at plenty at Phillips Academy if he came there like this in September.

He went downstairs and followed the smell of food down the hall, into a dining room with a big round table in the center and dish-filled sideboards on both sides. The table was set for two with a white cloth. His grandmother motioned to the big plate piled with baked chicken, baked potatoes, corn on the cob, and green beans. She said simply, "Eat. You must be hungry."

Paul was. He picked up his napkin, put it on his lap, and

13

fell to eating. His grandmother was a good cook.

When he was done, she told him, "You eat with a good healthy respect for food. There's no nonsense about you."

"I was hungry." Paul flushed. He should have talked to her while he ate—not just wolfed down the food.

"That's fine. I think it's a tribute to the cook to see people eat hearty. Now before we have dessert, which by the way is blackberry pie, I want to give you your present. I've got it right here. It's a sort of family heirloom, I guess." She pushed a box he had noticed beside her plate up to him. "Open it. It's your turn to have it. I didn't gift-wrap it."

Paul opened the plain cardboard box. There, on a bed of tissues, lay a big, gold-colored belt buckle. In its center was the outline of a heart formed by a line of deep red stones set a fraction of an inch apart.

As he stared at it, thinking how strange and gimmicky it was, Mrs. Weber said, "This is a man's belt buckle, Paul. I know it looks like a Valentine's Day present from a dime store, but it isn't. I think the stones in it are garnets. The buckle is very old. I remember seeing it when I was a child. I thought perhaps you'd wear it on the belt I got for you today. I chose that one specially for this buckle. Here, boys your age wear special buckles on their belts. I've seen them—silver and turquoise and all that sort of thing, and eagles and hawks, even the brand names of beer companies."

Paul took the buckle out and held it. It was heavy, heavier than it looked. Clearly his grandmother valued it, so he would have to wear the thing. He asked, "Where did it come from?"

"It belonged once to Billy Smart. Or at least, it was among his things."

"Who's he?"

Paul saw his grandmother's grin as she answered. "I never did know how he was related to our family, but he must have been. If he'd been born later he would probably have been another Hoot Gibson or Tom Mix or Hopalong Cassidy—or even John Wayne. But he was too early for the movies or television."

"He was a cowboy, huh?"

"More than just a cowhand. He was a rodeo star. He died years ago, long before your mother was born. Wear the buckle. Wear it for me. Lance owned it, too. He never wore it, though, because he worked in a bank while he went to college, and in the sixties bank tellers didn't wear western gear. It's high style now, though." She laughed. "The buckle wasn't the sort of thing Lance went for in any event—not even on his college campus. He aimed to be a professor someday." Now she reached out and touched Paul's hand and said, "No, I *don't* expect you to wear it back home in Delaware and shock your friends!"

Hearing this, Paul smiled. She did understand: she knew that he didn't take to the buckle any more than the sober-minded Lance probably had. It was sure gaudy. Well, he could and would wear it here for her sake. She had put on the peridot earrings already. He'd put the buckle onto the

15

belt tonight and wear it from now on. It wasn't as if the buckle had flowers on it. Yet the heart shape was bad enough. Why would a man buy a belt buckle with a big red heart on it?

Suddenly Paul thought he knew. Billy Smart probably hadn't bought it at all. Some woman had bought it for him a long time ago—some woman who'd liked him a lot. He might even have been some sort of idol. There were probably girl groupies in his day, too, who went for cowboy rodeo riders.

Paul said, "I bet this old Billy Smart had a lot of girl friends, huh?"

Mrs. Weber told him, "I have no idea. Perhaps he did. Perhaps he was the strong silent type who kissed only his horse. Do you think a woman gave him the buckle?"

"Uh-huh, I do."

"Lance said that once, too, come to think of it. He said it had to be from some woman who was romantically interested in Billy. Whoever she might be, she went to a lot of expense and trouble for him. That was made specially to order by a jeweler somewhere, not by some costume jewelry company. Well, Paul, I doubt if this did the lady any good, though. I do know two things about Billy Smart—he lived for a long, long time and he never did get married."

Paul set the buckle down and said, "Maybe Calamity Jane gave it to him and he got scared. I saw an old movie about her once. She'd scare anybody."

Mrs. Weber nodded. "Maybe Annie Oakley, the sharpshooter, did. Perhaps Billy could have known her. Oh, well, we'll never know for certain. Put it on your belt and let's see what kind of things it might bring to you. One thing for sure, people are going to notice you. You know, it intrigues me. It has for years. I know there's a story about it. Just you tell anybody who asks you that it's an old family heirloom. Maybe it's red glass, but the family has always claimed it's garnets and old Colorado gold. We never bothered to get it appraised because we didn't want to hear the stones were glass. It's more fun this way. Garnets are January's birthstone, did you know?"

"Yes, I did. That's the month I was born."

"I know. That's one of the reasons I gave you the buckle. They say wearing your birthstone brings good luck. So far as I know, you're the only January person in the whole family! Maybe you're the one who was to come along and wear it. Maybe it'll bring its secret to you somehow."

"Do you go in for ESP, Grandmother?"

"In a way. Sometimes I do, Paul. And sometimes I'm right, too."

2

NOT
WHAT WAS
THOUGHT!

At breakfast the next morning Paul's grandmother had a surprise of a different kind for him. When he came down at her call, he could hear her voice from the kitchen saying, "Oh, no, Phyllis, not today! My grandson just arrived yesterday. I really don't want to come to the hospital again today. Can't somebody else take that gift shop shift? . . . Oh, she's sick? Oh, all right . . . Yes, he's old enough. He's thirteen. He can look after himself. Paul's a big boy. He can start to explore this neighborhood by himself, and he and I will sight-see later. Yes, Phyllis, I'll be there at ten. Good-bye."

A moment later Sally Weber came in; she was wearing a

pair of tan slacks and a blue, African-pattern blouse. Frowning, she said, "Paul, I volunteer at a hospital every week. A lady's down with the flu, so I'll have to fill in for her at the gift shop cash register today. That leaves you here alone. I'm sorry this had to happen your first day here."

"Oh, it's okay."

He saw how her eyes surveyed him. She said, "The heirloom buckle looks just fine on you—not natural, but fine."

"That's good. Say, do you want me to call you Sally maybe, instead of Grandmother."

She laughed. "Neither of those, Paul. Grandma suits me to a T. Use that. I ate my breakfast already. Now I have to go change my clothes. I wear a striped uniform when I work for the hospital." Digging into her blouse pocket, she gave Paul a set of keys with the words, "These are to the front and back doors. Keep them. I've got another set. I'll go up and change now. Let yourself in and out of the house."

"Sure, Grandma."

Sally Weber pointed and said, "The public library's three blocks away in that direction. It's in a shopping center. It's a low brick building—you can't miss it. The video arcade's there, too. If you want a library card today, give my name as a reference. They know me there."

"Okay, but I'll go to the arcade first, I think."

"Whatever you want to do. Do you have any money?"

19

"Uh-huh, Mom gave me some."

Mrs. Weber paused in the doorway. "Paul, do you ever hear from your other grandparents?"

"Jesse's folks? Sure, they live in Vermont. They send me clothes and other stuff at Christmas time and on birthdays."

"No, I don't mean them. I mean your blood relatives, your father's people."

"Oh." Paul shook his head. "Mom used to hear from them sometimes at Christmas but after she wrote them that she married Jesse they stopped corresponding. She doesn't mind, and I don't either, really."

"I'm glad you don't, Paul. Some people in this world are beyond understanding. I've always had a lot of family feeling. Other people have very little. Are you still going to go to that fancy private school your parents signed you up for?"

"Phillips Academy? Yes, in September. It's the best there is around. It'll be hard but it's good."

She nodded. "Hard schools are the best. What will you do with your life? Will you be an engineer, too, like Jesse?"

"I don't know yet, but I don't like math a lot, so probably I'll do something that doesn't require a lot of math. Maybe I'll be a professor of English. I sure like to read."

"Like Lance, eh? You're a Weber. You look like him, you know." For a moment her face crumpled. Then she smiled and added, "That's fine, but I hear it's a long haul getting there."

"It sure is, but I like books a lot. When should I be home for supper?"

"Just before the sun begins to sink over Pike's Peak, or five-thirty if you prefer."

"Five-thirty's fine."

"Good. Take good care of Billy Smart's buckle, Paul. Don't let anybody talk you into putting it up as ante in a poker game."

Paul stifled a sigh as she left the room. Oh, but she was sure putting on the western act. He looked down at the gaudy buckle. Who would want it anyway? If he didn't know it was too much trouble, he'd take it off the belt before he left the house. It had taken some effort to get it onto the leather last night and he didn't want to go through that again. He'd wear the belt, buckle and all, and act as cool and calm as if he were wearing cutoffs and a polo shirt at Rehoboth Beach at home. He'd hope other buckles here were equally bizarre. One thing for sure, he'd keep his eyes peeled for what other dudes were wearing.

Paul ate his breakfast and waited until he heard his grandmother drive away. Then he rinsed the dishes and put them into the dishwasher. He went upstairs to get some money, came down again and went out the front door, locking it behind him.

The weather promised to be like that of the day before. No, he wouldn't need the windbreaker. He decided to walk to the video arcade first, and found the shopping center

21

with ease. It was a neighborhood one, with the same collection of stores known at home—supermarket, drugstore, boutiques, barber and beauty shops, real estate office, and a jewelry store. Though the buildings here weren't Colonial style, they looked much like the ones back east, except for the odd-looking, quivering trees planted on the mall.

The video arcade, though, was something to see. The building was designed to look like a tombstone, curved at the top like one made of white rock. The door was open and showed a dark hole, where lights of many colors constantly flashed and faded. The black-and-red neon sign on the outside said "Last Chance Games!"

Peering inside, Paul saw a few people at the rows of games. Yes, they were mostly kids his age, as his grandmother had said. He went inside and put a coin into one of the machines, a game with bug-eyed, green monsters chasing girls in space suits across a purple landscape on the planet Eldona.

As he played, he became aware that someone had come up beside him. Turning his head, he saw it was a girl his age watching the game with him.

A beam of white light from the ceiling lit up her long red hair and thin freckled face as she said, "That's a dumb game you've got. It's an old one. There are some new ones that are more fun to play. I come here a lot. I guess you're new here or you'd know about the new games."

Paul told her, "Thanks, but I know this game. I like it."

Suddenly she laughed. "You talk different. You sure aren't from here. Where are you from?"

"Delaware."

"Wow, that's a long way off. What grade are you in?"

"I'll be in the eighth grade in the fall."

"Me, too. Are you here for the summer?"

"Yes, just visiting."

"With relatives?"

"Yeah."

The girl said, "I'm Kelly Morse. I come here a lot with a friend of mine, Brian Holmes, but he hasn't come yet today. My dad's got a shop here in this mall."

By now Paul had decided this girl wasn't about to go away. She was a nosy kid, but she looked okay. She sure was friendly. Why not be friendly to her, too? Maybe she'd introduce him to some other kids his age.

As Paul stepped back from the machine a burst of clear bright light from the game hit his belt. The girl gasped and pointed at him. "Hey, that's sure a neat buckle you've got on your belt. Is that what kids wear in Delaware?"

Paul laughed and said, "No kid in Delaware would ever wear this. It comes from Colorado. My grandmother says it's old, and that the red stones in it are garnets, but she doesn't know for sure. Maybe they're just red glass. I'm wearing it to please her because I'm living with her this summer."

"What's your name? Would you like to know what they are for sure?"

"Paul Braun. How would I find out?"

"Ask my dad. When your game's over, come with me to his jewelry shop and let him look at your buckle. He can tell you, I bet."

Paul stared at Kelly. He said, "I don't know about that. That'd be appraising it, and I don't think I can afford to pay him to do that."

"Oh, Dad won't charge you. I'll ask him for you. Come on, you just lost the game. One of the monsters got hold of the last space girl. I hate that game. It's unfair to females."

They left the arcade and walked together to a glass-front shop a few doors away, with trays of rings and other jewelry displayed in the window. The window bore the gold-lettered words, "B.F. Morse, Jeweler, and P.M. Dobbs, Watchmaker–Repairer."

The moment he saw Mr. Morse Paul knew where Kelly got her red hair and freckles: she resembled her father. As he looked up at them, another man came forward from behind a low partition at one end of the shop and stood beside Mr. Morse. Seeing the green eyeshade he was wearing, Paul figured this short, balding man to be the watch repairer.

Mr. Morse asked his daughter, "Who's this, Kel? Need some more money for the video machines?"

"Not right now, Dad, thanks. This is Paul Braun. I've brought him here so you can take a look at his belt buckle. It belongs to his family. His grandmother says the stones in it might be garnets. Paul thinks they're red glass."

Paul told him, "It's supposed to be real, real old. Otherwise I'd say it's red glass out of busted car tail-lights."

This made both men laugh. Mr. Morse said, "Maybe it's better than glass. Take it off and let me see it."

Kelly spoke up fast. "Dad, Paul hasn't got any money, so please appraise it for him for free."

"Where have I heard those words before?" said Morse with a mock sigh, as he took the buckle Paul had just got off his belt and handed over to him.

The two men peered at the buckle together. Mr. Morse stroked and hefted it, then took it to the rear of his shop, where Paul saw him put something black into one of his eye sockets. After a time he called out, "Come back here, Pete, and take a look at this, will you?"

"Sure, B.F."

Paul watched Dobbs look at it, too, with one of the black eye-things. Then both men came back and Kelly's father handed Paul the buckle with a smile. He said, "The stones aren't glass and they aren't garnets, though that's what they appear to be. You're in for a big surprise. These are rubies, very old ones of an antique cut. The buckle itself is made out of heavy gold plate. Your buckle, I'd say, is about a hundred years old, give or take a decade or two."

"Rubies?" squeaked Kelly.

"Rubies?" muttered Paul, dumbfounded, staring at the buckle. "My grandmother's going to get a shock when I tell her. She's Mrs. Weber. She's lived here all her life and she thought these were garnets."

25

"Is she Sally Weber?" asked Dobbs.

"That's right. She's my grandmother."

Mr. Morse asked, "Would you be Kim Weber's boy?"

"Yes, do you know my mom?"

Morse replied, "Oh, sure, we both knew each other when we were in high school. She was the cutest blonde there." Morse turned to Dobbs. "You thought so, too, didn't you? You used to date her."

"Now and then." Paul saw Dobbs's shy grin. "Your mother was pretty popular. I doubt if she'd even remember me. A guy had to stand in line to date her." He turned to the other man to ask, "What's the buckle worth, B.F.? The kids are going to ask you that in a second anyhow, so I'll ask first."

The jeweler frowned. "Not much, unfortunately. The stones make an interesting pattern, of course, but they aren't big ones, and as I said, the cut's very old-fashioned and it doesn't bring out the brilliance the way modern cuts do. If I were to buy it to resell as antique jewelry, all I'd offer is around forty-five or fifty dollars. Do you want to sell it, Paul?"

"No, I don't want to, Mr. Morse. Grandma wouldn't want me to. It belonged to somebody in our family a long time ago, somebody she knew who died when she was a little girl, even younger than me."

B.F. Morse laughed and said, "That was before I was born. Whoever owned that must have been noticed wher-

26

ever he walked. Will you go on wearing it? It's a real con-
versation piece."

Paul looked at the red stones winking in the overhead
light of the shop. Rubies, he had heard, ought to blaze red
fire in a person's eyes; and if you turned the buckle just
right to the light, these stones did blaze. He said, "I guess I
will. Grandmother says it belonged to my Uncle Lance, too,
but he never wore it. I think she wants me to wear it while
I'm visiting for the summer. Did you know Lance Weber,
too?"

"I did," came from Dobbs. "We were the same sort—
had our noses in books all the time at school. I liked him."

"I knew him, too," volunteered Kelly's father, "even
though I wasn't close to him. Pete, you were in the same
outfit as Lance was in 'Nam, weren't you?"

"No, we were in different branches of the service. I was
Army, he was a Marine." Dobbs smiled ruefully at Paul,
shook his head, then went back behind his partition and sat
down to his work.

Paul told Mr. Morse, "Thanks a lot. I'll sure have something to tell Grandmother at supper tonight about Billy
Smart's old belt buckle."

"Who was he?" asked Mr. Morse.

"An old-time cowboy star Grandmother says she thinks
may be related to us."

Kelly asked, "She *thinks*? Doesn't she know?"

"No, she says not."

Kelly shouted, "Mr. Dobbs, have you ever heard of a cowboy actor named Billy Smart?"

"No," came the answer.

Kelly's father motioned to some papers on his counter and told Kelly, "Your mother's got relatives galore—second cousins once removed, whatever that means. I don't know them. Nobody in her family can keep it straight. It happens in families. Now you kids go on back to the arcade and let me get back to work here. It was nice to meet you, Paul. Maybe I'll see you again. By the way, where's your mother these days?"

"We live in Delaware, but right now she's in Athens, Greece."

"She travels, huh? Well, that's fine if you can afford it."

"Well, thanks for looking at my buckle, Mr. Morse."

Outside, Paul halted and put the buckle back on his belt as Kelly watched.

She asked, "Would you be scared to wear it if it was really valuable?"

"Yes. I'd tell Grandmother to put it in the bank, but it's okay to wear it." Paul patted the buckle and smiled. "Rubies grow on a person!"

Kelly giggled. "Liking rubies could grow on me real fast. Come on back to the arcade so you can meet Brian. He ought to be there by now. He's sort of my boy friend. He'll want to see your buckle. I bet he's never seen a ruby in his whole life."

Brian Holmes was standing outside the arcade. He was a

round-faced, thickset, brown-haired boy who, to Paul's dismay, was wearing cowboy boots and a straw cowboy hat. He stared hard at Paul as he came up with Kelly.

Kelly introduced the two of them, saying, "Paul's here visiting this summer from Delaware."

Brian had a loud voice. "And when the summer's over, you'll be going back to the East Coast, huh?"

"That's right."

Brian nodded as he looked Paul up and down. Then he pointed to the belt. "What's that for?"

"Nothing that I know about, except to hold up my jeans. It's a present from my grandmother. It . . ."

Kelly interrupted. "Brian, Dad just looked at it. The heart's made out of rubies, and the buckle's gold plate. It's real old. It's a family heirloom."

"Rubies?" Brian came closer to Paul to peer at the buckle.

Kelly went on. "Paul says the buckle belonged to a cowboy star, a relative who died a long time back."

"What kind of star?" asked Brian. "Singing? Movies?"

"Before movies—rodeos, I think."

"Rodeos?" Brian's blue eyes widened. "Maybe he got it as a prize for being top hand in a rodeo?"

Paul asked, "Wouldn't that be a silver cup?"

Brian scoffed. "Who can wear a cup? Prizefighters used to get belts with diamonds in them and they still do. Rodeo riders would get belt buckles. What was your relative's name?"

"Billy Smart."

Brian reflected for a time, then said, "I never heard of him. I'll ask my uncle who rides in rodeos if he ever did. Hey, Paul, do you like horses?"

Paul told the other boy, "I was never on a horse in my whole life."

Looking disgusted, Brian said, "Oh, a real easterner. Do you like sports? What kinds do you play?"

"Soccer, mostly."

Kelly put in, "Brian's goalie on our school team. It just won a state championship."

As Brian measured Paul with his eyes, he asked, "I bet you're a halfback, aren't you?"

"You're right—left halfback."

Kelly said, "Girls play soccer here, too. I'm a right half-back."

Talking soccer, the three of them went into the arcade. They spent the day together, eating cheeseburgers and wandering about the mall. Late that afternoon, as they parted to go home, Kelly and Brian gave Paul their phone numbers. Paul didn't know his grandmother's number yet, but he told them her name and address so they could look her up in the phone book.

At five o'clock Paul headed for home. He felt better about the summer ahead now that he had made two friends so easily. Colorado people didn't seem to stand on so much ceremony as Delaware folks did. By the end of the summer he might have even more friends. Kelly and Brian, who had warmed up to him more, had said they would help him meet others.

As he walked back to his grandmother's house, Paul glanced at the ruby buckle now and then. It had brought him good luck today, even though he now knew it wasn't his birthstone.

The moment Mrs. Weber came into the house Paul ran to her and cried, "Guess what, Grandma? The buckle's got rubies in it, not garnets like you thought. A jeweler's daughter I met today took me to her dad, and he looked at it and told me what the stones were."

"Rubies?" Mrs. Weber stopped still and shook her head in disbelief. *"Real* rubies? Why, Paul, nobody ever suspected the red stones would be rubies. My parents never did. Lance didn't. If we had suspected they were valuable stones, we certainly would have had the belt appraised ourselves. I wonder if Billy Smart knew what kind of stones were in his buckle. It certainly wasn't what we thought." She chuckled. "Well, if a lady gave it to Billy, she must have been crazy about him."

"I've got another idea, Grandma. Maybe it wasn't a lady at all. It could have been a rodeo prize. A kid I met today told me that."

"Perhaps it was. Well, isn't this interesting, though. My mother found the buckle among some of Billy's things up in an old trunk in the attic. We never knew exactly where it came from."

"Grandma, there's even more! Mr. Morse, the jeweler, said this buckle's at least a hundred years old. They don't cut rubies like this anymore. That's how he knows."

"A century old—perhaps even older? Well, well!" Mrs. Weber's face was perplexed. "Heavens, I would have said it came from around the time of World War One, when Billy was in his prime as a performer—1914 or something like that—not dating from long before I was born myself. None of us had any inkling it could be that old." She counted on her fingers, then nodded. "I must have been seven or eight when I attended Billy's funeral. People came to it on horseback. There were even Indians in feathers, as I recall. But perhaps I have it all mixed up with a parade I saw as a child. I don't know, Paul. But if the buckle is as old as the jeweler says, it must have been made around the time Billy Smart was a little child himself."

Paul said, "That would mean it belonged to somebody else in the family before him. If he was little, he couldn't wear it. Big belt buckles with rubies in them wouldn't be for little kids."

"Certainly not. You're right. Only a man would wear that, but I wonder who that would have been." She added with a smile, "Perhaps you'll find that out, too. Well, you have had a good day. You've had some fun with the buckle, and I take it you made a friend or two already."

Paul told her, "I made two friends. One of them's a girl."

"That's good to hear. Say, Paul, do you think you'd be

interested in looking through Billy Smart's old trunk yourself?"

"What's in it? Any more belt buckles?"

"No, just papers so far as I recall. I looked through it years ago just for fun, and all I found were some old scrapbooks and newspaper clippings, and some old photographs. I thought at the time that Billy was a handsome man. Anyway, I've thought for years I should clean out the attic and go through the trunk and the papers in it more carefully. I wanted your grandfather to get it down out of there, but he always found an excuse not to do it. He'd go fishing instead. It's a heavy old thing, so I let it stay."

Paul offered, "Maybe one of the kids I met today and I can do that for you."

"That'd be fine, Paul. If I ever give this house to the city, I'll have to clear out the attic in any event. I should probably give Billy's papers to the city library, too. You can help sort them out. . . . Come on now, let's you and your rubies march into the kitchen and help me start supper. Then I'm going to phone some of my friends and tell them that we're a lot richer than we thought we were."

"But we aren't, Grandma! The buckle's only worth about fifty dollars. That's what Mr. Morse said. I believe him."

Sally Weber grinned and flung up her hands. "Easy come—easy go. So we're not richer—but we *are* wiser: we know we've got rubies and we know that somebody must

33

have owned the buckle before Billy Smart got hold of it somehow. Maybe you've got the ball rolling on the buckle, Paul. There's probably a story there—if we're ever able to find it out—but it isn't likely that we will. Do you like your buckle now?"

"Yes, I do. I think maybe it's lucky."

"Good, I'm glad you like it, and I hope it will be lucky for you."

3

JAY

Kelly called Paul that night with an invitation. "Brian and I aren't going to the arcade tomorrow morning. That's when he plays water polo at one of the pools the Parks Department has. I sit and watch him play when I don't swim in the other pool. Do you want to come along?"

"Sure—where's the pool?"

"Six blocks away from the shopping center. Ask your grandmother to bring you. Bring trunks and a towel and fifty cents and . . ." Kelly hesitated for a moment, ". . . don't wear your belt buckle. The lockers there aren't so good when it comes to locks. They get busted into."

"Okay. I won't wear it. I'll go ask my grandmother if she'll drive me."

Mrs. Weber was watching the news on TV, but turned her head at the sound of Paul's footsteps.

Paul said, "That was Kelly Morse, the girl I told you about." Then he told her of his invitation.

"Of course I'll take you there, Paul. I know where it is."

"Thanks. Once you drive me there I'll get home by myself." He went back to the phone to tell Kelly that he could come, and to ask what time he should be there.

After they hung up, Paul came back and sat down beside Mrs. Weber. When the news was over, she turned off the set and asked, "Is Kelly Morse redheaded?"

"Yeah, she is. She's the daughter of the jeweler who looked at my buckle."

The woman nodded. "I don't know the girl, but all of the Morses I ever knew when I was growing up were carrot tops. They're a nice family. I have my watches and clocks fixed at Morse's shop by an old friend of Lance's, Pete Dobbs."

"I met him, too. Do you know Brian Holmes's folks, too? He's Kelly's boy friend."

"No, they must be new here, but the Dobbs family is an old one here in Colorado Springs. Like ours."

At ten the next morning, Paul got out of the Weber car at the pool with his swim gear, leaving his grandmother to drive to the supermarket.

There were three pools, one of them for small children,

all surrounded by a tall chain-link fence, and beyond them lay a cinder-block building. Around the pools were areas of bright green sod. As Paul walked toward the building he could see two water polo teams in the nearest pool. One team wore yellow caps, the other black. They were splashing and yelling. The next pool was for diving and general swimming. It, too, was noisy. Passing it, Paul was hailed by Kelly, who stood up and waved a green-and-orange towel at him to get his attention. She wore a green bikini. Paul waved back and went to the building to change into his swim trunks. After showering he went out to the pool where Kelly waited, lying on her towel on the grass.

She raised up on her elbows to tell him, "Hi! Brian's only just started the game. Do you want to swim now? I'm mostly basking today."

"Basking?"

"Yes, what lizards do to get their blood to warm up. You go swim, then come back and bask, too."

The water was cool, cool enough to shock Paul as he dived into it. He swam four laps, dodging little kids dog-paddling, and then heaved himself up out of the pool to lie shivering beside Kelly.

She wasn't alone now. Two girls her age, a blonde and a brunette, and a lanky, tow-headed boy had joined her. She introduced the girls as Tammy and Jennifer, friends from school, and the boy as Jason, her cousin.

Tammy and Jennifer were talkers, and so was Jason.

They said, "Hi!" then began to chatter about their school and the teachers, the band, and the various sports teams, shutting Paul out as if he wasn't there at all. The thought entered his head that if he had on the ruby belt buckle there would be something for him to talk about, but he wasn't wearing it. The other three didn't seem interested in his coming all the way from Delaware, and when he told them he would be attending Phillips Academy, they didn't seem ever to have heard of it.

Paul tuned them out. By now he felt warmed up by the sun, and drowsy, too, so he scarcely listened to Kelly and the others. Suddenly he felt Kelly's hand on his forearm and heard her call his name.

"Paul, wake up. Jay's here today. He's in the pool now. He'll probably come over here in a while."

"Who's Jay?" Paul lifted his head.

Tammy put her hand over the top of her pink-striped bikini and sighed, "Jay Jenkins, oh-boy, Jay!"

Kelly told her, "Oh, pooh! He's never even said two words to you, Tammy. He thinks you're a half-wit." Turning to Paul, Kelly said, "Ignore her." She pointed. "That's Jay going up the ladder at the end of the pool. He's going to dive. He's a great diver."

Paul rolled over, sat up, and shaded his eyes to see better. He liked diving. He saw a boy going up the ladder at the far end of the pool whose wet black head shone like a polo player's cap. Wearing a flame red pair of trunks, his body was brown-red from head to foot.

Jason said, "Jay's an Indian, a Ute. He transferred to our school last year. All the girls went nuts over him. He's a pretty good dude, once you get to know him—*if* you can get to know him."

An Indian? Paul had never met one. He surely didn't associate Indians with diving, but this Jay was, as Kelly had said, a "great diver." He watched the other boy go to the highest platform. Jay poised there for a long moment, then did a nicely executed double somersault, hitting the water cleanly. After that dive he confined himself to a series of jackknife dives, all well done, too. Paul noticed that many of the swimmers stopped in the water to watch him.

Paul told Kelly, "He's good, all right!"

"Would you like to meet him?"

"Do you know him well?"

"Well enough to ask him over. He and Brian are playing soccer together this summer when Jay can come."

Kelly got to her feet and walked to the other end of the pool. She bent over to talk to the boy in the water, and moments later she and Jay Jenkins came walking back together. Tammy, Jennifer, and Jason fell silent now. From closer up, Paul saw that the Indian boy was handsome. His dark face had a carved, angled look and his dark eyes were almond shaped and very bright.

As Kelly began the introductions, Paul got up politely to shake Jay's cold, wet, outstretched hand. Jay's voice was soft. "Kelly told me just now that you're from Delaware. I read once that the Delawares are the fathers of all the peoples."

Paul said, "Yes, it was the first state after the American Revolution."

Jay sat down cross-legged opposite Paul. "No, I'm not talking about that. I mean that the Delaware Indians, the Wabanaki, are supposed to be the oldest tribe in the whole country."

Paul asked, "Do you mean they were the first ones over the land bridge from Asia?"

"Yes, they followed the mastodons and mammoths. They called other tribes their 'grandchildren'—even the Mohicans. The Indians all say they were the first. The Delawares made peace between other tribes at war."

Paul said, "Wow! I didn't know all that. You're a Ute, aren't you? That's what Jason said just now. Is that a Colorado tribe?"

"Yes. There are also Utes in Utah. Why are you out here?"

"My mom went to Europe with my stepfather for the summer, so she sent me out here to stay with my grandmother."

"What happened to your real dad?"

Paul was taken aback a little by this boy's direct questions. He thought, I wonder if all Indians do that. Well, why not give a direct reply? He told Jay, "He dumped me and Mom when I was just a baby."

Kelly wailed, "Oh, Paul, that's awful! I know a girl that happened to."

Paul told her, "Oh, it's not so bad. Mothers can run out,

too, I hear, but my mom didn't. My stepfather Jesse's a
good dad. He didn't invite me to go to Europe, though, because he wanted Mom to himself. I understand."

Jay said, "My dad was killed in a car accident when I was
little. It happened on the reservation we lived on then. I've
got a stepfather, too. He isn't a Ute. He's white. He's gone
a lot."

Paul asked, "Is he good to you?"

Jay shrugged. "He's okay, but Mom wishes he'd make
more money so she wouldn't have to work so hard. He
doesn't work steady. He's gone to Texas now on a con-
struction job. Mom and I live alone with the Old One. She's
sort of like a grandmother to me. I mow lawns and have a
paper route early in the morning. I don't mind work. It's
okay. Do you work where you live?"

"No, not yet. Who's the Old One? My grandmother's
not an old lady."

"The Old One is some kind of aunt of my mom's. She's
so old nobody knows how old she is. She doesn't talk in
English much, only in Ute. What do you do if you don't
work?"

"Play soccer. Listen to music and stuff like that."

By this time Paul had become uncomfortably aware that
Tammy, Jennifer, and Jason were restless. Jay hadn't paid
them any attention at all. It was as if he and Kelly were the
only other people here. Now the others got up, mumbled
"See you later" to Kelly, and left, trailing brightly colored
towels to another spot on the lawn.

Jay asked Paul, "Do you like to read?"

"Yeah, I read a lot."

"What?"

"Science fiction. Sports stories, too. What about you?"

"Sure do." Jay smiled. His teeth were large and very white. "You don't jabber like a monkey like most kids around here. That's good. Most people talk too much and don't listen enough. That's what my mom says. Maybe I'll see you here again, Paul." With this, Jay got up, nodded goodbye, and left.

Paul was somewhat awed by Jay. After the boy left, he asked Kelly, "Are all Indians as serious as Jay is?"

Kelly laughed. "I don't know, but I can tell you that Jay sure is. He's sort of deep. I never heard him talk so much before to anybody. I think Indians don't generally talk a lot, especially to strangers. At least Jay doesn't. Hey, what'd your grandmother say when you told her about the buckle having rubies in it? I was going to ask you right off but you went in for a swim before I could."

"She was really surprised. She said nobody ever even suspected. She was also surprised to learn how old your dad thinks it is. That makes her think it wasn't made for Billy Smart at all. He wouldn't have been old enough to wear it a hundred years ago. Don't get mad, Kelly, but could your dad have been wrong about how old it is?"

"I don't think so. He's seen an awful lot of antique jewelry by now." Kelly flopped onto her stomach to nest her chin on her arms. She said, "That old buckle's neat! It caught my eye right off. But it gives me the shivers when I think of it."

"You mean it scares you?"

"Not exactly, but it's exciting—like the kinds of things you read about in adventure stories. You know, eyes of idols, ruby ones, being stolen out of Hindu temples. There's something evil about rubies. My mother says I feel things more than most people. That's good and bad, you know. I read that there are people who can just hold something old and tell you all about its history."

"If you know anybody like that, I'll let them hold the buckle. Do you read a lot, Kelly?"

"Uh-huh, I'm a bookworm. I don't read science fiction or sports stuff, though. I read romances and mysteries and history. I'm going to enter the summer reading game at the branch library. So is Brian."

"Brian likes to read?" This surprised Paul.

Kelly laughed. "You're surprised. So was my dad when I told him. Brian reads plenty but he keeps it quiet. He says he's entering the reading game just to get one of the prizes the library gives away, but that isn't the real reason. He likes to read books."

"Prizes?"

"Sure. They're giving a paperback book to every kid who reads and reports on ten books during the summer. But that isn't what's going to make kids read a lot this summer. They're going to read to get a chance at the governor's prize book."

43

"What's that?"

"A big book of pictures of Colorado scenery. You know, the kind folks keep on coffee tables to look at. The governor's going to autograph it for the kid who wins. A man on the library board is giving it as a gift. First, you have to read ten books, then you write an essay on something that happened in Colorado history. That essay gets you into the race for the governor's book. A history teacher at one of the colleges here and two librarians will read all the essays and judge them. The book goes to the kid with the best essay. All the branch libraries in the city have reading games, so a lot of kids will be entering the contest."

Paul rolled over onto his back and, shielding his eyes from the sun, said, "Well, that lets me out. I don't know anything about Colorado history since I don't come from here. My mom grew up here, though. She'd like to have a big book like that, but I can't write what I don't know about."

Kelly said, "Yes, that's too bad. Kids who live here would have a big head start on you. Well, you could enter the game for the ten books and the free paperback, couldn't you? I did last year, and got a neat prize. The Friends of the Library give out super paperbacks. Your grandma lives here and you live with her. You could get a library card through her."

"She's already told me that. I'll probably be reading some books while I'm here. Ten won't be much for me to read." Paul drew himself up to a sitting posture as he saw

Jay again on the high-dive platform. "Will Jay Jenkins write an essay?"

"He could if he wanted to. He's smart enough, I know. I was in a class at school with him." Kelly laughed. "As a Ute, he was here before your folks or mine came to Colorado. He ought to have plenty of ideas."

After Jay's splash, Paul said, "That was another super dive he just did. Who'll you write about, Kelly?"

"Women, pioneer women who wanted to vote."

"What'll Brian write about?"

"He says probably about famous old mines. His great-great-grandfather was a miner in Fairplay and his great grandpa mined, too."

"Both of those ideas sound good to me."

Kelly nodded. "I'll be going to our neighborhood library in the afternoons now to look up stuff I can use. Brian, too. We want to start work on our essay ideas while we're reading our ten books. Some of the books I read for the paperback prize will be for my essay. You can find us there in the afternoons if you want to, Paul."

"Jay, too?"

"He comes there sometimes. You heard him say he has to work."

"Where does he hang out when he isn't here at the pool?"

"He mows a lot of lawns up and down Twelfth Street most afternoons, and some mornings, too."

"That's pretty close to where my grandma lives, isn't it?"

45

"Yes, it is. Maybe he mows her lawn, too."

"No, I saw her gardener this morning real early. He's an old guy."

Suddenly Kelly stood up to wave, and told Paul, "Here comes Brian. It's halftime in the game." She whispered, "He's probably mad that I didn't watch him every minute he played, but he'll get over it. Look at him stomping. He doesn't look to me like his team's doing so well." She sighed. "Brian's sort of jealous of Jay because he's such a good diver and he said no to Brian about playing on the water polo team. Jay only does what he wants to do, not what other people want him to do."

Paul stayed silent, thinking. That's how he was inside, too—like Jay. He hated to be pushed by anybody, to be told to do what they wanted him to do. Maybe that's why the Indian boy interested him—they were the same type of person.

4

THE
TRUNK
UPSTAIRS

The first thing Paul told his grandmother as he went into the kitchen on coming home was, "I met a real Indian today. He's a Ute. His name is Jay Jenkins. I liked him."

"Good." Mrs. Weber wiped wet hands on a towel. "The Utes owned a lot of this state at one time. I've known some Indians over the years. They're shrewd, intelligent people. I like the way they live with nature. Bring this boy around sometime, and those other children, too. Now tell me about the rest of your day."

"Well, I heard about the library summer reading game."

"There's one every summer, Paul."

Paul shook his head. "Not like this one. Kelly Morse told

me that there'll be a reading game and if you finish that, there's an essay contest to win the governor's special book."

"Really? What would that be?" Sally Weber walked over to the sink to rinse the lettuce.

"A big book of photographs of places in this state, the kind of book Mom likes so much."

"Tell me all about it while I fix the salad."

As he leaned against the refrigerator, Paul repeated what Kelly had told him. He finished with, "I guess I'll read the ten books while I'm here, but I can't enter the essay contest. I don't know enough about this state's history."

Mrs. Weber cocked an eye at him. "You could study up on it. It's only been a state since 1876. That gives you a hundred years less history to cover than for the thirteen colonies. Gold was discovered here in the 1850s."

"Before then only Indians lived here?"

"Just about, plus some mountain men and fur traders."

Paul shook his head. "From 1850 till now is still a lot of history. I'd have to read lots more books than the ten, even if all ten I read are about this state."

"That's probably true, and some of the books would be hard sledding for somebody your age. I see your point. Well, anyhow, try to make at least one of your ten books about my state, to please me."

"Sure, I'll try to find one I like. I'm going to meet Kelly at the library tomorrow. Will you go with me so I can get a card?"

48

"Of course I will. I have some books to return anyhow."

Paul met Kelly waiting on the front steps of the library the following day. She had been waiting for Brian but decided not to wait any longer. After Paul introduced her to Mrs. Weber, she went in with the two.

At the counter Paul got a temporary library card for visiting patrons. Then he and Kelly went into the young people's section, where Kelly introduced him to the librarian, a red-haired woman with gold-rimmed glasses. She signed Paul and Kelly into the reading game and showed them the huge, hand-drawn map on one of the walls. It was of Colorado Territory before 1876. There were cut-out pictures of old miners with picks, Indians, gamblers, and cowboys on it as decorations, and lines representing roads that went north and south, east, and west across the map.

"These are old stagecoach routes to Denver and other towns," the librarian explained. "Each book you read puts you farther along the road. When you've read all ten, you come to your destination and get your prize. I'll give you a card so you can keep track of your books, and we'll keep your progress marker here. It's a tiny, colored stagecoach with your name on it. I'll move it farther along the road you choose with each book you read. Ten moves get you to where you want to go." She smiled and added, "You can tell where you and your friends are by how their coaches move along."

Paul was wearing the ruby-studded belt buckle, and now Kelly pointed to it. "Look at that, Miss Haskell. It's real rubies. It's plenty old."

The librarian nodded. "Yes, I saw it. It's very colorful."

Suddenly Kelly punched Paul on the arm. "Hey, I just had an idea!" She turned to the librarian. "Miss Haskell, where would we look up old-time Colorado cowboys? I mean rodeo performers, real big old-time stars."

"Go to the reference desk over there and ask if they've got a book on old Colorado notables, or an old *Who Was Who* in the state or country."

"Okay. Thanks, we will. Paul, let's get some books and then let's look up the old guy you say used to own your belt buckle."

Fifteen minutes later Kelly and Paul, carrying two books apiece, came to the reference desk. A young, brown-bearded man sat frowning behind a long desk, his eyes intent on a large book open before him.

Kelly poked Paul. "You talk to him. It's your family, not mine."

The librarian looked up. "Yes?"

Paul told him, "Miss Haskell said you might have some books on Colorado notables. I have a notable I want to look up."

The man smiled. "Yes, we do. Some of them are even mug books."

"What're they?"

"Books with portraits, photographs. Old time notables

50

liked to have their pictures in books. They don't do that so much anymore. I'll show you where they're kept."

As the librarian got up and came around the desk, Kelly explained, "Paul wants to look up a man who may be a relative of his, who used to wear the belt buckle he's got on now. It has real rubies and it's real old."

"Rubies, huh?" The librarian stopped to look at the buckle. "My hobby's researching Colorado history. Do you mind my asking who the original owner of your buckle is?"

"Billy Smart," said Paul.

"Smart, huh?" The librarian smiled and said softly, "That happens to be my last name, too. I'm Matthew Smart. Is your name Smart?" he asked Paul.

"No, it isn't. It's Braun, my stepfather's name. I'm not from Colorado. I live in Delaware. I never heard of anybody in my family named Smart, and neither has my grandma—except for Billy Smart. Grandma remembers him from the time she was a little girl."

Kelly asked, "Mr. Smart, are you from Colorado?"

"Oh, yes, my family's been here a long time now. Come on. I'll show you where the books are. Good luck in your hunting. When and if you find your Billy Smart, come and show me. I know he's no ancestor of mine because my mother does genealogy work, but I'd like to know about him anyway—for the sake of the name."

When he'd gone, Paul and Kelly pulled several big books down from the shelves and started to look through them. What a bunch of whiskery, mustached, hair-parted-in-the-middle dudes, thought Paul. There were dozens of them in the "S" section, but no Billy Smart.

Finally there was only one book to go, called *Centennial State Worthies.* Paul looked through it while Kelly mumbled over another one. On page 432 Paul found something—a piece about four inches long, about a William Smart, also known as Billy Smart and as "Bronco Billy" Smart. There was no photograph to go along with it. No death date was given for him, but there was a record of his birth, March 15, 1872, in Colorado Springs, Colorado Territory. There was no name given for his mother or his father, nor for a wife or any children, as had been listed in other entries Paul had seen.

He whispered to Kelly, "I found him. I got him! He was still alive when this book was put together. Let me read it to you. 'Mr. Smart is a circus rodeo performer of considerable note. He has traveled widely in this country and in foreign climes. He is considered one of the most valuable performers in the Wild West shows sponsored by William Cody, who expresses a great deal of confidence in Mr. Smart's abilities and values him as a friend and colleague.' "

"Cody?" Kelly's eyes were popping. "Paul, that means Buffalo Bill Cody. What else does the thing on Billy say?"

" 'Mr. Smart, who is renowned for his courtesy, chivalry, and modesty, is a credit to the state he represents.' "

"Paul, is that all it says?"

"Look for yourself."

Kelly looked and shook her red head. "This is funny.

Look at all there is on these other people. I guess Billy Smart was too modest to give out much information about himself. He couldn't have been so modest if he went around with Buffalo Bill, though, and if he wore a ruby-studded belt buckle. Come on—you lug this over to the librarian, Paul."

Juggling his own books, Paul took the fat tome to Matthew Smart, who read the entry and said, "Well, this is a start. There are books on Buffalo Bill here and at the main library downtown, too. You could go down there and perhaps find out more about Mr. Smart." He grinned. "And because he and I have the same name, I'll try to do some further looking for you in vertical file materials—old clipped papers, I mean. Some are indexed enough for me to do that without too much work. Would you like me to try?"

Paul said, "Sure, please. I would. I'll drop by and see if you've got anything when I come back to get new books for the reading game."

"Fine. Before you go, give me your name and phone number so I can call you if I hit real pay dirt."

"Pay dirt?" asked Paul.

"Real gold," explained Kelly with a sigh.

Paul said, "Call my grandmother's house. She's Mrs. Sally Weber. She's in the phone book."

"Ah, I know her, and I know the house. I've visited many times. My mother has known her for years. They play bridge together. Knowing your grandmother gives me even more reason to hunt up your relative, Billy Smart. I'll even put your request in our library newsletter to see if anybody knows of him. What relation is he to you anyway?"

Paul laughed. "I don't know. Grandma doesn't know either. Thanks, I really appreciate your help. Good-bye."

Paul and Kelly found Mrs. Weber sitting in the library lounge. She was reading as she waited for them. Paul said, "I've got something to tell you."

After greeting Mrs. Weber, Kelly excused herself. She said, "I've got to go back to the kids' part of the library to find Brian," and she was gone.

When he and his grandmother were in the car going home, Paul told her what he had found out.

She said slowly, "I never dreamed that Billy rode in Buffalo Bill's famous Wild West Show. I always thought he was just a rodeo performer. Or perhaps I was told about Buffalo Bill a long time ago before I knew who he was and I forgot." Suddenly Mrs. Weber reached out and grabbed Paul's knee. "Paul, you can enter that essay contest, too! You've got something to write about—Buffalo Bill and his show and Billy Smart. You won't have to use the library much. You've got lots of raw material for an essay—Billy's trunk up in the attic and his scrapbooks. That ought to tell you some interesting things. See what you can find. Something might even turn up there about the ruby buckle."

"Would there be stuff in there about Buffalo Bill?"

"I'm sure of that. He was one of Colorado's most famous sons of all time. I read once that his Wild West Show was world famous in its day. Buffalo Bill performed for kings and queens and presidents. You might have a real gold mine

54

up in the attic. Perhaps there are even photos of Billy wearing the ruby buckle. I know there are old photographs in the trunk, but I don't recall what they were."

As Paul looked straight ahead, he realized that he was getting excited. How much stuff would there be in the trunk? How big was it anyhow? Some old trunks he'd seen in movies were large enough to put an elephant or a moose into.

As Mrs. Weber started down a side street, Paul suddenly cried out, "Hey, stop, please. I see somebody over there I want to talk to. Jay, the Indian boy I met yesterday, is mowing that lawn. I can get home by myself. I know the way."

"All right, Paul."

Mrs. Weber stopped the car, and Paul jumped out and ran up to Jay. The other boy nodded as Paul began to keep him company walking behind the mower. For a few minutes they followed the noisy machine, then Jay reached down and shut it off.

He told Paul, "I can talk for a couple of minutes, but then I've got to get back to work. I have two more lawns to do this afternoon."

"This won't take long. I just wanted to ask you if you're going to be in the library reading game and the Colorado history essay contest, too. I am."

Jay said, "I know all about the game and the essay stuff. But I haven't got time for it this summer."

"You ought to try to enter, Jay. Being a Colorado Indian, you ought to have a lot to write about!"

"Maybe so." Jay scratched his nose, then he pointed to Paul's belt and asked, "What's that?"

"A belt buckle somebody in my family used to own. It's got old rubies in it. I'm going to write about the old guy who used to wear it. It belonged to Billy Smart, who used to perform with Buffalo Bill's Wild West Show a long time ago."

"Hmm, Buffalo Bill?" mused the Indian boy.

"Yes, my grandma says there's a whole trunk of papers about Billy Smart in her house. Are you sure you don't want to enter the reading game and the essay contest, too?"

"Maybe. I'll think about it."

"Oh, go on and do it. You could write about Indians."

"I might." Jay's eyes flashed at Paul. "There might be something in your trunk about Sitting Bull, the Sioux chief. I read about him. He was in Buffalo Bill's Wild West Show for a little while. People booed him, but Buffalo Bill gave him a circus horse that did tricks and a big white cowboy hat. There were other Indians with Buffalo Bill, too. Would your grandmother let me look at the papers?"

"Sure. She asked me to ask you over. Would you write on Sitting Bull, then?"

"Maybe. I like the idea."

Paul went on. "I want to find out what I can about this old belt buckle, too, if I can. It isn't worth a lot of money, but it's over a hundred years old."

Jay nodded and bent to start the mower again. Over its

loud sputter, he yelled, "I'll come to see you Sunday afternoon. I know where you live—in that big old white house
that looks like a cake. If you look in the trunk and find anything about Indians, save it for me, okay?"

"Sure. If I do, will you write an essay, too?" Paul shouted
in return.

Jay didn't answer, only smiled. Paul stood watching as
the Ute strode away from him following the mower over
the lawn. Then he started for home along the sidewalk,
thinking about Billy Smart's trunk and wondering what
might be inside it.

A half hour later Paul followed his grandmother up a
narrow stairway that led to a brown door. She opened it and
preceded him into the attic, then pulled a dangling chain to
turn on a light. As she did, she said, "I haven't been up here
for a long time. What a mess this place is!"

Paul, who lived in a new house and had never seen an
attic before, agreed. This was a big, musty-smelling place
filled with old-fashioned lamps and shades, a lady's dress
form, old chairs and scarred tables, cardboard boxes,
trunks, and other luggage of various sizes. One trunk was
huge, almost as tall as he was. It had labels on it that said
"London," "Paris," and "Rome."

Pointing to it, Paul asked with a sinking heart, "Is that
big green one Billy Smart's trunk?"

"Good heavens, no. That's mine. It's a steamer trunk
from my honeymoon abroad. His is the brown one with the

leather straps and curved top. When I was a child, I thought that it was a pirate chest. I imagined there would be pearls and diamonds and emeralds and sapphires and maybe even gold coins in it, but the only thing of any value was the buckle you have on. The rest of it is paper."

They went over to it together, but Mrs. Weber didn't open it. She waited a moment, then told Paul, "You open it. It's your adventure. It's a man's whole life in there—all that's left of Billy Smart. Some people leave children, all others leave in the end is paper. But at least Billy did make his mark in the world." The woman's hand squeezed Paul's shoulder, then she turned and left the attic.

5

THE
OLD
LETTER

Slowly Paul lifted the lid of the trunk. It had no top tray, and he peered down into a jumble of disarrayed papers. Once more his heart sank, for they looked as if a whirlwind had gone through them. This was going to be a big job!

How should he begin it? Paul thought hard. One way would be by the dates on the things. There ought to be dates on letters and bills, right? Should he start first on the scrapbooks or on the loose paper? Perhaps the scrapbooks would be the best. They ought to go along in chronological order, too.

Paul picked up a piece of yellow, folded paper on the very top. It was a receipt for a silver-mounted saddle and bridle that came to $40.43, dated 1903. So Billy Smart had bought some fancy horse gear that year! It must have been a big purchase for him to have kept the receipt. Paul wondered if he would find other sales receipts. They'd be dull stuff for an essay.

Pushing aside rustling old paper, Paul got out the four scrapbooks. He decided to take these down to his room, where the light was better. Leaving the trunk top open, he turned off the attic light, went down the stairs to his room, and set the musty-smelling scrapbooks on his bed.

Before he could start on them, he heard his grandmother's light footsteps at his open door. She came in with a big black book in her hand. "I heard you come down," she said. Her gaze took in the scrapbooks and she nodded, then continued, "I looked in this old family Bible for an entry for Billy Smart. The dates go way back to the 1840s. There is one for him, but . . ." She was frowning hard.

"What's the matter?"

"I don't know. Billy is there all alone—sort of out in left field. He's the only Smart in the whole list of people. I can figure out the relationships between the other people listed, but not Billy's. It says, 'William Smart, born March 15, 1872, died March 23, 1930.' I have no idea who entered his name and the date of his birth, but the handwriting is old and very flowery. The date of his death is in my mother's hand. I recognize it very well."

Paul ventured, "Maybe he was adopted by somebody in the family? But he's out in left field, like you say." Paul pointed to a place in the right-hand margin where two very different handwritings were visible. It appeared to him that Billy had barely made it into the Bible at all.

Mrs. Weber sighed. "I don't look in here often. Your mother's name is here, and Lance's, too. The last name of all is yours. When the time comes, this will be your mother's. She'll be the one to write in the dates of your marriage and when your children are born."

"Oh, Grandma!" said Paul, embarrassed.

"I mean it. Someday you'll have this, too. In the old days, the names of all the family—uncles and aunts and children—and the dates of their births, marriages, and deaths went into the big family Bible. Bibles were used to record such important dates as death and birth certificates before hospitals existed. I'll take this downstairs for now. I'll call you when supper's ready. It's in the oven now. Go ahead, look through the scrapbooks. It's your adventure."

Somewhat embarrassed, Paul asked her, "Did opening the old trunk make you sad?"

"In a way it did. The attic depresses me a little. There are memories stored up there of your grandfather and Lance and my parents. It makes me lonely to go up there, so I almost never do. It's good to have you here with me this summer, Paul. I hope you like being here."

"Sure I do. I didn't think it would be this interesting, though."

"Yes, it seems to be getting deeper and deeper for you, doesn't it? You start with a belt buckle we all thought contained garnets, and now you end up researching the life of a man who seemed to have a claim on our family. I think you've only started to 'mine' Billy Smart, Paul. You could be bringing him back to life in a way."

Paul shook his head. "That would take a lot. I sure don't know much about him right now. By the time I get through his trunk, though, we might know more than we wanted to know."

She chuckled. "You mean that he might have led a wicked life? No. A lot of people came to his funeral, remember, so he must have been likable to have a lot of friends. I've got to go now and put the peas on to cook. I'll give you a yell when supper's ready."

That night, at his uncle's old table, Paul started through the most tattered of the scrapbooks. On its first page he saw Billy Smart's signature for the first time. It was tall and spiky, with a flourish under the entire name and a sketch of a roweled spur at the very end to finish it.

Paul grinned. He liked the spur in the signature. Maybe that was Billy's trademark. At least it wasn't a heart like the one on his buckle. That would be a dumb thing for a male rodeo star to use.

There were a lot of papers in the scrapbook. Some were yellowed, faded old newspaper clippings that he could scarcely read. Some were drawings. But there were no photographs. Occasionally Paul found a date, but usually not. One of the first was 1896. It was printed on a line drawing of a bucking horse. Below it Paul read the faint words,

"Bronco Billy Smart, famous 'trick rider,' on Fifty Cents."
He laughed. That was a weird name for a horse.

Halfway through the scrapbook he found a sketch of two
people, one of them a man with long hair and a goatee
wearing a fringed buckskin coat, broad hat and high top
boots. Paul guessed this was Buffalo Bill Cody. Beside him
stood a short, plump woman in boots, a fringed buckskin
skirt and wide hat. She held a rifle at her side. Paul read,
"Buffalo Bill and Miss Annie Oakley, Miss Sureshot."
Annie Oakley? Paul wished he could read the smaller print
below that, but it was blurred. He could see from looking at
the covers of the albums that they'd all got wet at one time
or another. Maybe some other things in the trunk had also
been wet. That would make it even harder to decipher Billy
Smart's stuff.

Near the end of the scrapbook Paul found more drawings—this time of Indians in feather headdresses. He
smiled. This would interest Jay. He put a slip of paper to
mark the place in the book, finished looking at the last few
pages, and went on to the next one.

That scrapbook wasn't any use to him at all. Except for
some pages toward the middle, none of the newspaper articles was in English. Paul guessed from what Mrs. Weber
had said that these were all clippings about Buffalo Bill's
Wild West Show from foreign countries it had visited.
Those in the middle were from England. There was a
drawing of Queen Victoria beside a fancy western-style
saddle with figures of buffalo heads on it. The article under

the picture said that it was a special saddle the queen was giving Cody, the great American frontiersman. The other articles in English were about the various performers in the show, among them Annie Oakley, trick rider Bronco Billy Smart, and some Indians. Once more, Paul put in a slip for Jay so the boy could read this for his own essay.

The third scrapbook contained mostly photographs. The same man appeared in most of them, so Paul figured he was Billy Smart. He was short, dark haired, and light eyed. In almost every photograph he wore western clothes—old-time cowboy outfits, but fancy, too. There were no childhood photos of him; the album started when he was a young man. In the first photograph Billy Smart stood with his arm around a woman in a big plumed hat and fur coat. She looked older than he was. Under it was written simply "Ma and me, 1891." Other photos were of him on horseback, and some with him standing up on the backs of two horses. In others he was smiling with Buffalo Bill and other show people, or sitting at a long, white-covered, bottle-strewn table with people Paul didn't recognize. None of these pictures had writing on the back. One early photograph showed Billy Smart wearing a fancy wide belt that covered most of his middle like a cummerbund. A prize belt? Paul peered hard at it. No, there wasn't a heart shape there— just a mass of metal and what looked like white stones. In two later pictures, he wore fancy belts, but neither had the buckle Paul was looking for. The boy sat thinking. There hadn't been a buckle with a heart on it in any of the draw-ings or photographs of Billy. He was dead sure of that.

As Paul turned the pages of the album, Billy Smart grew older. In the last section he was middle-aged, and on the last page he was barely recognizable, because he was wearing checkered pants, a derby, and striped shirt—a clown's out-fit. Had he become a circus clown? No, not that! As Paul stared at the backgrounds of the photographs, he saw that there were horses and riders in western gear. A rodeo clown! That's how Billy had ended his career.

The last scrapbook had only two pictures. They were both of Billy in his clown suit. In one he was sitting on a corral rail, and in the other standing with his arms around the neck of a burro. The rest of the pages were blank. These must have been the last photos ever taken of him.

As Paul brushed his teeth for bed that night, he thought of Billy Smart, wondering what he'd been like. The Wild West Show clippings had told him what Billy had done for a living and what had made him famous for a time, but not what the man himself was like. Paul wanted to know. After all, if he was in the family Bible, Billy Smart was probably related to him. Maybe he would find out more about the cowboy star when he looked through the rest of the old trunk's contents.

The next morning Paul brought the scrapbooks to his grandmother in the kitchen and set them on her counter.

She asked, "Did you find anything interesting?"

"Quite a bit of stuff. Would you look, too, please? There are a lot of photographs and drawings of Billy, but he never wears a heart buckle in any of them."

"Sure, I'll look, too. You might have overlooked it."

Paul frowned. "He ended up as a clown. I guess that's sort of a comedown from being a real performer, isn't it?"

"A clown?"

"Sure, look at the last pictures of him. Here in this album."

When Paul showed her the last photographs, Mrs. Weber began to laugh. She said, "He was a rodeo clown. That's something very special you wouldn't know about. A rodeo clown's more than just a funny man. He's a daredevil. He keeps wild Brahma bulls away from bucked-off riders while they're on the ground. The clown gets the bull to chase him. He's sort of like a matador in a bullfight except he doesn't have a cape and sword. Rodeo clowns are very brave men—and very fast, too."

"Hmm," Paul mutttered. Then he said, "After breakfast I'll hook a lamp up and look through the rest of the trunk."

"You'll be up there all day long."

"Probably I will."

"You like this, huh?"

"Yeah, I do." He smiled. "I'm glad Billy was a rodeo clown, not a funny clown."

"Paul, do you think you'll get an essay out of old Billy?"

"I dunno yet. I want to try, though."

She patted his belt buckle. "Okay, I'll bring you up a sandwich for lunch. Is tuna okay with you?"

"That'll be fine. I like tuna."

By midday Paul was halfway through the trunk, unfolding, reading, and setting what he found beside him on the attic floor. So far he'd found only old receipts for clothing and other things Billy had bought, and playbills and posters for rodeos and shows. There were no letters, birth or marriage certificates, or any of the sort of things his mother had said most people kept in bank vaults the way she did.

At noon his grandmother brought him a sandwich and a big glass of milk. She asked him, "What have you turned up?"

"Not much. There isn't any birth certificate, so I can't tell who his father and mother were."

"That's not surprising. In 1872, when Billy was born, babies were born at home, not in hospitals. That's why family Bibles were very important, and as reliable as today's records. Good hunting, Paul!" And she was gone.

The rest of that day Paul went through the remainder of the trunk's contents. It offered pretty much the same type of mementos. Some of the papers were dated; most were not. At four o'clock, his eyes tired, Paul came to the very bottom of the trunk. He sat on his stool, pondering its emptiness. Well, he could at least write an essay on the famous Coloradan who went from being a cowboy champion to a Wild West show performer to a rodeo clown. It wouldn't include much Colorado history, but it might be interesting, and it would please his grandmother. And his mother, too. He'd keep a copy of it to show her.

As he got up to leave and stood over the trunk, his eye was caught by a narrow rip in its stained leather lining. Something shone light in the rip. Paul reached down, widened the tear, and pulled out an envelope. It was tattered, ivory-yellow, and water-stained. There was no postmark—only the words "For Him," in thick black handwriting.

Paul carefully extricated a folded piece of paper from the envelope, then sat down and opened it, laying it across his knee to read.

It was dated July 30, 1872, in Colorado Territory. It was a short letter, written in the same heavy handwriting as on the envelope. On one side, at the bottom, there was a drawing of a heart. Opposite the sketch was a large blank area.

Paul Braun read the letter aloud.

My baby boy,

I hear tell you got born. I wish I could come have a gander at you but I'm keeping mighty busy. May be I'll come see you someday even if your ma spreads the word to folks we both know that she don't favor me no more. Its my hope you grow up good. There's a present for you along with this letter. I had it made special for your being born when I was in Denver. This is a thing folks who know me real good remember me by. There's something else in this letter for you to find out what it is. May be you'll get some use out of it too the way I have.

Your loving pa,
Frank Hart

Hart? The name had not been mentioned in any of the other papers. Paul's mind galloped. Hart—and the heart shape on the letter! Was the present from "your loving pa" the ruby-studded belt buckle? What else had Frank Hart sent with the letter? Paul felt carefully along the rip for anything else hidden beneath the lining, but there was nothing. What could the "something else" in the letter be?

Paul sat staring at the letter for a few minutes, then slipped it back into its envelope. Putting it into his shirt pocket, he turned off the lamp and hurried downstairs to find his grandmother. He wanted to show her this letter. He was pretty sure that he was the only one beside Billy who had ever seen it. It seemed to have been hidden in the lining of the trunk and he sensed that it was Billy Smart who had put it there. Billy had also packed away the ruby-studded buckle. Well, why would he do that? Paul sure had some questions to ask his grandmother. First of all, *who* was Frank Hart?

Two minutes later the exclamation "Frank Hart?" and the surprised look on Mrs. Weber's face told him that she had never heard the name before. When she read the letter, she said, "I don't know about this, Paul. Was the present that came with the letter the belt buckle? Was Frank Hart Billy's father? I've never heard of any Harts in the family. Well, let's go back to the old Bible."

They were soon poring over the handwritten old pages, going back and forth around Billy Smart's entry. As Sally Weber had said, there were no Harts listed. She took a pencil and a sheet of paper and, referring to the Bible often, made a chart starting with Paul himself. Working back through the generations, she put in his mother and herself and her husband, Paul's grandfather. Then she penciled in her own mother, Louisa; her grandmother, Marcella; and her great-grandmother, Indiana-born Lucy Ann Pettis, adding both their maiden and married names. None had wed a Hart. Next to Lucy Ann Pettis, Mrs. Weber wrote the names of her great-grandmother's brothers and sister. Lucy was born in 1854, her brother James in 1852, and Luke in 1849, and a sister, Sophronia, was born in 1850. Sophronia Pettis had married a John Blake in 1879. Mrs. Weber pointed to that Bible entry. It was a messy one and appeared to have been scraped with a pen knife and then written over. On each side of the name "John Blake" was a gray streak of ink on the paper.

Mrs. Weber told Paul, "I bet the old steel pen point that wrote that entry spattered ink. Pens did that in the old days." She closed the Bible with a sigh. "Whoever he might be, Mr. Frank Hart is not listed here. This Bible originally belonged to Lucy Ann, who started it with herself. I remember hearing that she and her brothers and sister came to Colorado Territory five years after the Civil War ended. That makes it 1870."

She thought for a moment and said, "The baby boy in the letter doesn't have to be Billy Smart. Nor does the present have to be the buckle."

"Then why would Billy have kept the letter and the buckle in his trunk?"

"I don't know, Paul. We may never know."

"Maybe not, but we've got the name 'Frank Hart' to work on now. I think I'll do some detectiving."

"You mean detection work?"

"Yes, that's right."

"Will you ask your friends to help you out? After all, they're native Coloradans. It could also make them better friends to you and give you more social life this summer." She touched his hand. "My dear, you need company your own age. I was delighted when I heard you would come here to me for the summer but I worried that you'd be very bored. The friends I invite here are mostly women my age. I don't really know their grandchildren. Do ask your friends to help you with the letter. Do you want to ask them to dinner some weekend soon?"

Paul thought a moment, then said, "Jay said he'd come over Sunday afternoon. He knows where we live. I think he's the smartest one. He'll have some ideas about this. Besides, he's the most Colorado one of them all. His ancestors were here way, way back."

"Good. I'm glad Jay's coming. Later, we can ask him and the others to a backyard barbecue."

"Grandma, there are some other people I want to show this letter to besides Jay and Kelly and Brian. Maybe the librarian, Mr. Smart, will know something or can find out something about Frank Hart. Maybe Kelly's dad or the guy who fixes watches with him might have heard the name, too."

"Yes, those are good ideas. Try them, of course. Maybe one of them can come up with something I can't. I'll also ask my friends if they ever heard of a Frank Hart. I know plenty of folks descended from pioneer families. And if I ask them to, they'll ask other people in their own families what they might have heard about him."

"Thanks, Grandma. While you're at it, ask 'em what they know about Bronco Billy Smart, too."

"I'll do that. Are you going to write about him?"

"Yes, I think I will," he answered enthusiastically.

Paul found himself surprised at how excited he felt. He'd never dreamed Colorado could turn out to be so interesting so fast. It sure was different here. And Jay wasn't one bit like the kids he knew at home. Jay was part of the interesting difference.

So was the ruby-studded buckle. Paul saw now that his

mother's family was tied tightly to the history of this state. And so was he—he was a Weber, too. Yes, he wanted to learn more about Bronco Billy Smart, who could be a relative of his!

6

KID RUBY?

Jay showed up at the Weber house at two o'clock Sunday afternoon. He was wearing good clothes, even a necktie. Paul could tell right away that his grandmother was impressed with the Ute boy.

Once they were upstairs in Lance's old bedroom, Paul showed Jay the places in the Billy Smart scrapbooks that had to do with Indians. Jay pored over them, nodding and smiling, pleased to see newspaper sketches and photographs of the chiefs who had been in the Wild West Show. He told Paul, "Long ago, newspapers couldn't reproduce photographs, so they used drawings instead, even though photography had been around since before the Civil War."

"I didn't know that."

"Most people don't. Are you going to write about Billy Smart?"

"Yes, but there's something strange about him. Look at this letter. I found it in his trunk." Paul gave Jay the letter.

After reading it, Jay shook his head as Paul slipped the letter back into its envelope and put it on top of the bureau. He told Paul, "Smart and Hart! They rhyme. There's a heart on the letter and on your buckle. That could have some meaning. They all sort of fit together, but I don't see how. What about the other thing the letter talks about?"

"I couldn't find anything else. I really looked the old trunk over, too."

Jay shrugged. "I guess you'll never know, then. After all, it had a hundred years to get lost in."

"Jay, have you decided if you're going to write an essay for the contest?"

"I think I might. Anyhow, I'll start on it and hope I can finish it."

"Are you still thinking of writing about the Indians in the Wild West Show?"

"No, I think I've got an even better idea. It's an old mystery that happened here in Colorado. I think I'll write about the stagecoach that disappeared in the Indian Peaks area back in 1873."

"Disappeared? A *whole* stagecoach? But they were so *big*!"

"That's right, they were. They were big things made out of wood and iron and leather, and were usually pulled by

75

four or six horses. Stagecoaches carried a guard and a driver plus passengers. This one had four horses, five passengers—and forty thousand dollars in gold aboard."

Paul whistled. *"Wow!* And all that stuff disappeared?"

"Yes, into thin air. Nothing ever showed up—not iron or bodies or anything at all."

"It sounds like science fiction—like a spaceship gobbled it up."

Jay laughed. "Yes, that's what we'd think today, but that's not what people believed in 1873. People then said my tribe, the Utes, attacked the stagecoach and that we made away with everything.

"When the coach left Colorado Springs for a mining camp seventy miles away, the news went out over the telegraph, so the miners expected it. The gold was for their payroll. But the stagecoach never got there. Both the army and some U.S. marshals looked high and low for the coach or any traces of it. They searched all the Ute camps, too, because they thought we did it. But they could never prove anything because they didn't find a single clue. Some of the old Utes remember hearing their grandparents talk about how the army and the marshals looked around—how bad they treated us."

Jay grinned. "The army and the marshals were sure upset about it. The route that old coach took was between rock cliffs almost all the way. There weren't any lakes or swamps or crevasses to fall into. Well, I'd like to write about this mystery, to tell how the Utes were suspected, and how they were treated, but with my summer jobs I don't know if I'll have the time to do any research on it."

Paul volunteered. "I can help you. My essay will be easier because I've got all this stuff right here on Bronco Billy. I can go to the library with you. At the same time, I'll see what I can find out about Frank Hart."

Jay said, "Thank you, Paul. Sure, I'd like to have you help me if you want to. What'll you call your essay?"

" 'Bronco Billy Smart, An Old-Time Cowboy Star.' What about you?"

"I'll call mine 'The Ghost Coach.' "

Paul felt a prickle at the back of his neck. "That's spooky!" he said.

"So's the disappearance. They never did find the coach. People looked for it for years—mostly because of the gold on it. But today most folks have never heard about it. I wonder if your grandmother has."

When Mrs. Weber was asked, she only shook her head. "No, I never heard about this, but it was way, way before my time. Seven people and four horses simply vanished, and as you say they had little time to vanish in! Why, Jay, the very idea gives a body goose bumps. When will you boys start working on your projects?"

"Detectiving," corrected Paul. Turning to Jay, he asked, "When can you?"

"Tuesday and Wednesday mornings, I guess. I haven't

got lawns to mow then. And any day it rains. We'll have to go to the downtown library, though. That'll mean bicycles. I've got one. Can you get a bike, too?"

Paul turned to his grandmother, who said, "No, there isn't one here, but my next door neighbor's son has a bicycle, and he's away for the summer. I'm sure she'll let you borrow it. It's an old ten-speed, but it'll get you there."

Jay told her, "My bike's old, too. That's good. We won't have to worry so much about them getting stolen. That's one of the funny things about the stagecoach that disappeared—the idea that the Utes would steal the gold on it. They didn't have a lot of interest in gold then. Even if they'd known what to do with it, the minute they tried to spend it the army would have been right on top of them. Indians are smart, smarter than they used to get credit for being. They couldn't use the coach. Nor were the passengers any good to them unless they held them for ransom, and that never happened or the Utes would have been caught at it. It's sure some mystery—and a mystery to my people, too."

Paul said, "It's a lot bigger mystery than mine about Frank Hart and Billy Smart."

Changing the subject, Jay now asked, "Do you want to play some soccer, Paul? There's a park not far from where I live. I saw Brian and Kelly there when I rode over here. It's not a real game, but we can kick a ball some even if there probably won't be two full teams playing. I'll go home and change my clothes first, though, once I show you where the park is."

Mrs. Weber told Paul, "You go on. Play as long as you want to and don't worry about getting dirty. I'll keep dinner for us. I don't mind." She asked Jay, "Would you like to come back with Paul and eat with us?"

"I'd like to, but my mom will expect me to come home. She wants me to write to my stepdad tonight. He's in Texas."

"Ah, yes! Paul has to write his mother and stepfather tonight, too. He's to write them in care of American Express once a week. I promised Kim that you would, Paul."

"Once a week—that often?" cried Paul.

"Yes, and it isn't as if you haven't got anything to tell them. Now, Paul, you go up and change your clothes, too, while I call my neighbor about the bike."

As the two boys left the house together soon afterward, Jay said, "My stepdad's named Jesse, too. That's interesting."

Paul asked, "Jay, have you got an Indian name?"

"Uh-huh. Jay Little Horse. I don't use it, though. Thanks for not laughing when you heard it. I don't like it when people do."

"I don't laugh at people's names or the way they look or talk. I only asked because I'm interested in you and your tribe. I like learning new things. Hey, did Utah get its name from the Utes?"

"Yes, they lived there."

The woman who lived next door to Mrs. Weber hailed the two boys, and said to Paul, "Your grandmother just called me and asked if you could borrow Michael's bicycle. That's fine with me."

Paul went with her into her garage, and she showed him her son's old bike.

After he thanked her, Paul and Jay cycled to the soccer field. The Indian boy left Paul, but soon returned in everyday clothes, and for a while they played soccer with Kelly, Brian, and a few other boys and girls. At one break in the game Paul told Kelly and Brian about the material he'd found in the old trunk and about Frank Hart's letter.

When he finished, Kelly said, "Hey, Paul, I bet my dad would like to see that letter. He might know about a Hart family living here in Colorado Springs."

Jay told her, "The letter said Colorado Territory, not Colorado Springs. That meant a whole state then."

Brian told Jay, "Yes, but there wouldn't have been so many people in it in those days. But you're right, it could have been written in Denver or anywhere."

Recalling the wording of the letter, Paul said, "No, it probably wasn't from Denver. Hart only said whatever he sent was *made* there. If he wrote it from Denver, too, I think he would have said so. I want to look Frank Hart up if I can."

Kelly laughed. "I wonder what the other thing enclosed

in the letter was. Maybe a diamond-studded teething ring for the baby."

"You're crazy, Kelly, even if you can boot a soccer ball," came from Brian. He turned to Paul, "Kel and I will be going to the downtown library pretty soon. We've found out just about all we can at the branch. Do you want to come with us when we go? The big library's the place to look for Frank Hart. Tomorrow's the last day we're going to the branch." Brian now asked Jay, "What are you going to write about?"

"Indians and a stagecoach," he said, and told the others of his project.

By the time the Ute boy had finished, Kelly Morse had her hands on both sides of her face. "Wow, Jay! A whole stagecoach plus all those people—and gold, too! That's something I'm going to tell Dad and Mr. Dobbs about at supper tonight. Mr. Dobbs is coming over." She laughed. "Mom's trying to match him up with a real-estate agent friend of hers. Mom's getting them together but I don't think it'll work."

Jay smiled, "My mom does that, too. She's trying to get Lewis Scarfe together with a friend of hers named Naomi."

"Who's Lewis?" asked Paul.

"A friend of mine. He's a Ute, too. Maybe you'll get to meet him. He lives a couple of houses from me. He goes to college, and he's real smart. I think I'll ask him to help me with my essay, too, like you are, Paul."

81

Brian asked Paul, "You're going to help Jay?"

"Yes, he has to work and I don't. He can't go hunt up stuff as often as the rest of us can plus read the ten books to qualify for the essay contest, too."

"That's nice, Paul," said Kelly. "If you come to the branch library tomorrow, bring the Frank Hart letter. Afterward we'll show it to Dad and see what he makes of it."

"Sure, I'll come to the library and bring it."

Looking at the setting sun, Jay said, "This Indian says Delaware brave go home now on cycle to grandma wigwam." He pointed to Paul and everyone laughed.

As he threw one leg over the top of the bike, Paul answered, "This Delaware brave go home. Delaware brave will see Ute brave who dives into cold water later in big tepee of books in big part of village." And he rode off, leaving Kelly and Brian groaning.

The next morning Paul found Kelly and Brian among the Colorado history books looking up pioneer women and old mines.

Kelly came over at once to whisper to him, "Nobody at dinner last night had ever heard of a Frank Hart, Paul."

That didn't surprise the boy. After Kelly went back to her books, he went with the Frank Hart letter to the librarian, Matthew Smart. Smart read it, then said, "This is interesting. Frank Hart, hmmm? The name doesn't ring any bells with me, but I don't know everything about old Colorado. I wonder about your belt buckle, and the names Smart and Hart. If Billy was Billy Hart, why change to Smart? Hart's a perfectly good name. It isn't Rumpelstiltskin, for instance. Take care of this letter. It's interesting and could be valuable if we can identify Frank Hart."

Paul said to Matthew Smart, "Oh, do you think so? I'll keep it in my room along with the buckle from the trunk."

"Why don't you come back later next week and see if I've learned anything about Smart and Hart. I've got some other research projects right now that come ahead of this. Meanwhile, why not try the name Frank Hart where you found the piece on Billy Smart?"

"Sure, I will. Thank you."

Paul spent the rest of the morning hunting under the letter "H," where previously he had hunted under "S." He found some Harts and Hatfields and Hartleys and Hartfords, but nobody named Frank or Franklin or Francis Hart who would have lived around 1872.

At noon Kelly and Brian came up to him with their notebooks to ask what he had found out.

"Nothing about Frank Hart. I'll start in again this afternoon on Jay's stagecoach. I thought I'd get old Frank out of the way first. The coach is bigger than he is."

This joke made Brian hold his nose, but Kelly said, "We'll eat lunch and then go see Dad, if you want to show him the letter."

"Did you ask him about the stagecoach, too, last night at your dinner party?"

"Uh-huh, but everyone said that they'd never heard of it.

Dad thinks it's some old legend that an old-timer made up. He says they used to tell some real whoppers. Maybe it's a Ute legend that Jay's fallen for. Neither Dad nor Mr. Dobbs believed it. They said if it's really true they would have heard about it. But Dad says that he's interested in what we're doing because it exercises our brain muscles. And to keep him posted. He likes history and he likes whoppers. Anyway, Paul, he's real interested in your old belt buckle. He's bought and sold a lot of antique jewelry that was made here in frontier times. So please show him the letter that goes with the buckle."

"Kelly, I don't *know* that the letter goes with the buckle!"

"But it's got a heart on it, and there's a heart on the letter, and it's written by a Frank Hart. So it does!"

Brian had gone on ahead of them, and now called back, "Let's go eat at the taco stand. I'm too hungry to stand around and talk about stuff that happened a hundred years ago."

After lunch the three went to Mr. Morse's jewelry shop. Paul gave him the letter to read. As B.F. Morse spread it out on his counter, Dobbs looked over his shoulder.

"Well," said Kelly's father, "this is intriguing. There could be a link between Hart and Smart, since you found this in a trunk belonging to Billy Smart, but how would you ever prove it?"

"I can't. Grandma and I looked in the old Bible that lists our family's names, but there aren't any Harts in there.

84

Billy Smart is, but all it says is when he was born and when he died."

Brian volunteered, "Could he be adopted? My little sister is."

"That's what I thought, too. We don't know."

Mr. Morse told Paul, "Let me know if you find out anything more about this. Or about that stagecoach. Last night Kelly told us about the Ute kid's idea about it. I never heard of that either and neither has Pete, here."

"Nope, I never did. I don't believe it ever happened," said Dobbs, as he returned to his work table.

Paul Braun found nothing that afternoon about Frank Hart or the stagecoach. He came home discouraged and that night called Jay with the sour news. "I didn't find a single thing. I asked the librarian about your coach and he said he had never heard of it before. Neither did Kelly's dad."

Jay told him calmly, "We'll go to the downtown library tomorrow and look in old newspapers on microfilm. Have you ever done that?"

"No."

"I know how. I did it once with Lewis. I'll be at your house at nine. All right with you?"

"Sure, Jay."

Cycling together, the two boys rode downtown the next day to Cascade Avenue and the big main library. Jay knew where to park the bikes and where to go to ask for microfilm. He was handed several cardboard boxes for 1873, containing old filmed newspapers of that year. Then the boys went into a small dark room with a row of machines in it. Jay turned on one, threaded the spool of film into the top of the machine, then pulled up two chairs and set them side by side.

Paul complained, "My gosh, Jay, we'll be looking at a whole year of newspapers! It'll be hundreds and hundreds of pages."

"No, Paul. Lewis told me that, long ago, papers were only a couple of pages long. While I turn the crank at the side of the machine to move the pages along, we'll look for anything about the missing stagecoach and Frank Hart."

Starting with January 1, 1873, the two boys sat hunched over the viewing screen, scanning every page. There was nothing of interest to them until the June issue of that year. Then suddenly there it was—the account of a stagecoach that was missing! It traveled three times a week between Colorado Springs and Fairplay, and then one day it had *disappeared*!

Paul and Jay both drew in their breaths. They read the story eagerly. The news piece listed the names of the passengers, driver, and guard, and told of the gold aboard. For days afterward there were follow-up stories of searches made by the U.S. Army and law officers, as well as speculations about the disappearance. The paper accused the Utes of committing the crime, as well as such outlaws as the Reynolds and the Devil's Head gangs, and Kid Ruby and his gang. According to the papers, nobody ever found the coach, and by the end of June there were no more stories about it.

In the July 1873 issues there were a string of stories about Colorado Territory's desperadoes, describing them as much as possible and listing their crimes. There was quite a bit about the Reynolds and Devil's Head gangs, but the paper gave only a very sketchy picture of the outlaw called Kid Ruby. A member of his band who was caught and hanged had told the sheriff only that "Ruby" was his leader's name, and nothing more about him. The paper went on to say that Kid Ruby always wore a wide hat and a long rain slicker or duster over his clothing, and a bandanna over his face. No one had ever seen his features!

"Kid Ruby?" breathed Paul, touching the ruby-studded belt buckle as he did. He whispered to Jay, "These are real old rubies, a whole heart of them. The name on the letter was Frank Hart, and he said he was sending something like what he wore and was known by. Could it be a buckle like this—I mean, the thing he was known by? Hey, what if Frank Hart was this Kid Ruby, and his men knew he wore a buckle like this one?"

Jay said, "I thought of that, too, but Ruby could be a last name, too. Let's look some more for articles about the coach and Kid Ruby."

The pair of them read on, but nothing more appeared about either topic until an entry dated very late September, when a reporter wrote that Kid Ruby seemed to have

87

dropped out of sight in the Territory. An editorial on the same page said, "Good riddance to Kid Ruby! Let us hope he's gone to his just deserts or to Arizona Territory to fry out there."

"Just deserts?" mused Paul.

Jay laughed, "I think they wanted him to go to hell and roast there—and if he didn't go there, to go to Arizona Territory where it gets awful hot, too."

Because Jay had hurried and mowed more lawns than usual the day before, he had the afternoon free. The two boys went back to Paul's neighborhood for a leisurely hamburger lunch, then to Mr. Morse's shop, where they thought they might find Kelly and Brian. They were there, as Paul had figured. Kelly introduced Jay to her father and the boy told him and Dobbs what he'd found in the old papers about the missing coach.

When Jay finished, Morse shook his head. "Hart and heart, and Ruby and rubies. Well, maybe. I dunno, kids. I never heard tell of a Kid Ruby, though I have heard of the old Reynolds gang. How about you, Pete?"

"No, me neither."

Jay told the men, "I'm going to mention him anyhow, to make my essay more interesting." He turned to Paul and asked, "May I copy Frank Hart's letter?"

Paul nodded. "Sure, you can copy it if you want to, I guess. It's still on top of my bureau. But why would you want to use it?"

"So I could ask if Frank Hart and Kid Ruby were both the same dude."

Paul said, "I'd planned to put it in my essay! I found the letter!"

Mr. Morse was grinning now. "Why don't both of you use it? Paul, you could ask if Frank Hart was Billy Smart's father and why Billy took another name. Jay, you can wonder about Frank Hart being the Ruby Kid. You could both use the same guesses and set up a mystery for the people who read your essays. Nobody can answer those questions, but then, not all questions get answered. Lots of historians raise unanswered questions in their writings. It's an acceptable thing to do."

7

THE
OLD
ONE

Mrs. Weber was at home when the boys arrived. Paul saw that she seemed pleased at Jay's coming back again so soon, and that pleased Paul. He was growing to love her more and more. He had to admit something he'd never believed possible—that maybe he wasn't missing out so much on Europe after all. Of course, he'd be going to see museums and castles and cathedrals there, but he'd be listening to Jesse or some tour guide tell him what he was seeing and what he should be thinking. Here in Colorado he was doing things for himself and doing his own thinking. No, that wasn't quite right. He was doing them with new friends, like Jay.

Jay went up with Paul to his room, copied the Frank

Hart letter exactly as it was written, examining it and the buckle with great, frowning interest, and then putting both back slowly on top of Paul's bureau.

Sally Weber was waiting for them when they went downstairs. She told Jay, "I wish I could ask you to stay to supper, Jay, but Paul and I were just invited out. We're going to Mrs. Smart's—she's the mother of the librarian you met. We've got a couple of hours before we have to get dressed for dinner. Helen Smart's very formal. She'll want to see you in a necktie, Paul. Jay, please sit down and tell me a little about yourself." She smiled at him.

"What did Paul tell you already?"

"Not enough."

Jay shrugged. "There's not a lot to say. My real dad was a Ute. He's dead. My mom's a Ute, too, though she's married to a white man now. I was born on the Ouray Reservation. It's named after a Ute chief. I went to school there for a while. We just came here last year—my mom and stepdad and the Old One. I guess the Old One must be about a hundred years old. She was a relative of Chipeta's."

"Who's that?" asked Paul.

"The wife of Chief Ouray. The Old One's related to my mom, too."

Mrs. Weber said, "That makes you a sort of prince then?"

"Oh, I don't think so. Ouray's not part of my family. Would you like to hear more about the history of my people?"

"I would," came from Paul.

Mrs. Weber put in, "Me, too."

Jay leaned back in his chair. After a moment he said, "Before the Spaniards came, nobody had horses. Indian horses either ran away from the Spanish or were stolen from them. Very long ago, my people wandered around on foot and used bows and arrows to hunt deer. We Utes called outselves Nunt'z, the People. We lived in the Rocky Mountains once we had horses, and fought against many different Indian tribes. Later on, we fought against the white man, too."

Paul's grandmother told Jay, "That's something I've read about. Jay, I've also heard that some of the Indians have beautiful religious beliefs."

"I think the Utes did. We believed in a god of war and of peace and floods and thunder and lightning. The real old people believed that when a Ute died, that person's soul was fought over by a bad spirit and a good one. Usually the good spirit won and the soul went with it to the Happy Hunting Ground."

"That *is* fine, Jay."

Jay looked at his shoes but didn't reply. Paul could sense the other boy's embarrassment at the compliment. Jay probably felt he had said too much. Paul understood. He did that at times, too. But after all, his grandmother had asked the question.

Suddenly the Ute boy got up and told them, "I guess I'd better get on home now. It's getting late." He flashed his shining grin at Paul and asked, "Are you going to wear Billy Smart's ruby buckle to that dinner party you're going to?"

Before Paul could reply, Mrs. Weber did. "He certainly is *not* going to wear that buckle! Tonight Paul is to wear a jacket and a tie. He'll hold his slacks up with another belt."

Jay was still grinning. He told Paul, "Your grandmother is a *wano momets.*"

"What's that?"

"A good lady. Ute for a strong one."

"Why, thank you, Jay."

The Indian boy now excused himself, saying he had errands to run for his mother, and left.

As Paul and Mrs. Weber went with him to the front door, Paul asked his grandmother, "Will that librarian be there tonight?"

"I have no idea. I didn't ask Mrs. Smart. I don't know whom she has invited. I doubt if you'll find anybody your age there. She has no grandchildren. She wants to meet you because she knew your mother and Lance as children. Perhaps you'll have a dull time. Life is full of dull times. But I can promise you one thing—good food. She's famous as a cook. Her desserts are wonderful."

This made Paul laugh. "That reminds me of something Jay said on our way over here. When old-time Utes ate with white men, the Utes always ate the dessert first and the main course afterward. I've wanted to do that lots of times when Mom cooks liver for dinner."

Sally Weber put her arm around Paul's shoulders. "That strikes me as a good way, if not a healthful one, to start a diet. Fill up with sweet stuff first and lose your appetite. Tell me, Paul, what did you and Jay find out in the library this morning?"

"We found some old newspaper articles on the coach. No one has ever found it, I guess. Nobody we talked to this afternoon seemed to have heard of it or of Kid Ruby. We found out he was an outlaw in 1873. Jay and I wonder if maybe Kid Ruby is Frank Hart and if maybe Frank Hart or Kid Ruby had my buckle made for his baby boy, Billy. Maybe Billy took the name Smart because he didn't want to have Hart as a name because of his father. Or maybe his mom gave it to him. It's a lot of maybes, huh?"

"Too many for me. Now, let's go up and get dressed, Paul."

"Mr. Morse says Jay and I can put those 'maybes' in our essays."

"I don't see why not."

After showering for the second time that day, Paul put on gray slacks, a pale blue oxford cloth shirt, and a striped gray and blue tie. He looked down at the jeans he had just taken off. They weren't too clean now. They deserved to go into the hallway dirty-clothes hamper. Getting them ready for the washer, Paul unthreaded the belt through the loops, took off the old buckle, and set it on top of Frank Hart's letter on the bureau. Then, whistling, he got out his navy blue blazer and started downstairs, dumping the jeans in the hamper on the way.

He found his grandmother in the living room, all dressed up for dinner, too. She looked pretty in a pale green dress that was pleated from top to bottom. Her shoes matched its green and so did her peridot earrings. She smiled and asked, "Ready, my handsome young prince?"

"Ready, fairy grandmother."

"Then let's get into our coach and be gone."

The bearded young librarian, Matthew Smart, was at his mother's house when Paul and his grandmother arrived, but Mrs. Smart, a plump gray-haired lady, told them that he was only there for a before-dinner drink. He had a dinner date himself. Mrs. Smart sounded put out with her son for not staying, thought Paul.

Matthew soon singled out Paul from among the other guests. He said, "My mother phoned this morning that she had invited you and your grandmother here tonight. Are you wearing that fancy belt buckle? If you are, let's show it off and give the ladies a jolt. My mother will scream."

"No, I didn't wear it." Paul smiled. "It is pretty awful, isn't it? I left it home. Grandma said I was to dress up tonight."

"Yes, my mother likes things gussied up for her parties. I don't dress up very often, but when I do I go all out. I learned about three-piece suits—like the one I've got on—

when I went to library school in the East."

"Do you know Delaware? Do you know Wilmington?"

"No, I was in Massachusetts most of the time. I never got any closer to Delaware than Philadelphia."

"I've been there lots of times."

Smart went on, "I liked the autumns in the East. Colorado's different in the fall, but beautiful, too."

Paul said, "I won't be here to see one. I'll be home then."

"But while you're here you plan to enter the summer reading game at the library, and I hear that you plan to enter the essay contest, too. I know plenty about you. Your grandmother and my mother talk on the phone a great deal. What will you write about?"

Paul told him, "Billy Smart. Bronco Billy Smart was his nickname. I read about him in a trunkful of old papers Billy had. You saw the old letter that was in there, too—the one Frank Hart wrote. Well, if Bronco Billy had been in movies, he would have been a real big star. I looked up Frank Hart in the downtown library this morning. I didn't find anything on him, but my friend Jay Jenkins and I found stuff on the old stagecoach that disappeared in 1873 and about an outlaw called Kid Ruby. We wonder if Kid Ruby and Frank Hart weren't the same person and if the ruby-studded buckle doesn't have something to do with Kid Ruby and Billy Smart. Grandma agrees it's a lot of maybes we've got going."

"It certainly is. As for Billy Smart, some people come

along at the right time. Others are too early or too late to fit their eras. He missed out on the movies. Good luck on your essay, Paul. I hope you win the prize."

Saying that, Matthew Smart smiled and left Paul to go over to his mother, who was beckoning to him with a crooked finger. Soon after, Paul saw him leave the house.

As his grandmother had warned, the dinner party was dull. Besides Paul, the guests included his grandmother and four other ladies her age, plus two men who were as old as the women. They all knew one another well and talked about things that had happened forty years back, about people they all knew and he didn't.

Paul asked one of the two men once, "Have you ever heard of anybody who lived a long time ago here in Colorado named Frank Hart? Did you ever hear of Kid Ruby?"

The man thought for a moment as he stirred his coffee. "No, never did. Sorry." He asked the whole table Paul's question, but they all shook their heads.

Mrs. Weber then asked the men, "Have either of you ever heard of Bronco Billy Smart?"

There was no response to that question either, but when she told of Billy Smart's being a rodeo clown, one of the men said, "Why, yes, I saw him at a rodeo when I was a little boy. He was brave as a lion. You should have seen him handle those wild Brahma bulls. I thought he was wonderful. He was supposed to be one of the best rodeo clowns in the entire country at that time, as I recall."

On hearing this, Paul felt a glow of pleasure and—yes—of pride, too.

Paul and his grandmother went home at ten-thirty. Bidding her goodnight on the stair landing, Paul went into his bedroom, feeling tired. He turned on the lamp by the bed, yawned, then took off his blazer. After he hung it up, he went over to the bureau to look in the mirror while he untied his tie. A casual glance at the top of the bureau made him gasp in shock. *It was gone! The ruby-studded buckle and the letter along with it!*

Paul looked to the open window, seeing its curtains blowing in the wind. Could they have blown off? He searched the floor beside the bureau, then peered under it. No buckle—no letter! He went to the window and looked out. Just out of sight below the windowsill was a tall ladder. But it had been on the other side of the house that afternoon!

Suddenly, Paul realized what must have happened. Someone had moved the ladder to his window, climbed up and come into his room, and taken the buckle.

Who could have taken it? Who had known he was going out tonight and wouldn't be wearing the buckle? Who would know where he kept it? And why would the thief take the letter, too?

The answer came clear as a fire engine bell. *Jay!* Jay knew he was going out; Jay knew he wouldn't wear the belt;

Jay knew where he kept it. Jay Jenkins, the person he'd begun to think of as his best friend here in Colorado! Jay had copied the Frank Hart letter, but that wasn't good enough. He wanted the real one along with the ruby buckle.

Anger blazed in Paul Braun. He ran to his grandmother's bedroom and knocked hard on her door. She came out at once, looking alarmed. "What is it, Paul?"

"Somebody's been here while we were out. Somebody took my belt buckle."

"Oh, my Lord, they could have ransacked the house! We'd better go see."

"Is your room okay?"

"I think so. Let me look in my jewel box first and then we'll go downstairs and look at the silver. How did the burglar get in?"

"He used the ladder that was on the other side of the house and climbed in through my window. I'm sorry, I left the window open to get some breeze inside."

"You should have kept it locked, Paul. Well, too late now. Come on, let's go down and see if anything else has been taken."

Fifteen minutes later Mrs. Weber and Paul had checked her room and the rest of the house for losses. There were none. The silver was all there, and so was the antique bric-a-brac. The few valuable pieces of jewelry Mrs. Weber owned were all accounted for. There were no signs of anyone trying to get through the doors or other windows.

Paul sat down on the stairs with his grandmother and told her somberly of his suspicions. "I've been double crossed. Jay took the buckle and the Frank Hart letter, too. It had to be him. He knew where I kept the buckle because he'd been in my bedroom."

"Oh, Paul, that's a sad thing to think."

"Well, it's what I *do* think. Other people knew about the buckle, but they didn't know I was going out tonight and wouldn't be wearing it. And they don't know where my room is, either. Only Jay knew all those things."

The woman nodded. "That's true. It looks bad for Jay." She sighed and patted Paul's hand. "I could call the police and ask them to come over, but I don't think I will. The buckle isn't worth much, and nothing else is missing. Well, you've still got that trunkful of Billy Smart material for your essay, and you can remember the contents of the letter, I'm sure. You've read it over so often by now. You won't be seeing more of Jay, I imagine."

Paul growled, "You bet I won't see him! He wanted my buckle bad enough to steal it from me. I didn't think he was that kind of guy."

"Tell you what, Paul, I'll drop by the police station tomorrow morning and give them a description of the buckle. It's too bad we didn't take an identifying snapshot of it, but I never thought to. Anyway, it's so odd a piece that if it ever shows up, the police will know who owns it."

Paul shrugged. "It won't ever show up, Grandma. We

might just as well forget it—the way I'm going to forget Jay. I won't help him look up stuff on the disappearing coach. I don't need to go to the library much. I've got most of what I need right here in the old trunk."

"That's right, you do. You don't even have to mention the buckle or Frank Hart's letter if you don't want to. You can concentrate on Bronco Billy, the rodeo star. If you'd like, I'll try to round up some older people who might have known him or have seen him as a rodeo clown. Would you like that?"

"Yes, thank you."

Paul didn't sleep well that night for thinking of Jay—who had come treacherously to his house and stolen from him. He was finished with the Ute boy. He'd tell Kelly and Brian only that some burglar had taken the buckle, not that Jay Jenkins had. He couldn't prove it. Since Mr. Morse knew about old jewelry, he might keep an eye open for the buckle if he ever saw it for sale somewhere or read a description of it. Maybe Jay would sell it. Even if it were only worth fifty dollars, they seemed to need money in his house.

He came down late to breakfast, and as he nibbled at his food, Mrs. Weber told him, "I've been on the phone to the neighbors. The lady who lives across the street and two doors down had a break-in last night, too, while she was out to a movie. She lost a Georgian silver teapot and a cloi-sonné box. She said that the couple next to her had a pair of very old Chinese porcelain vases taken. So, if it was the same thief as ours, he was after antiques, but he didn't know the value of antique jewelry very well. The lady who had the teapot stolen said she called the police, but they weren't able to do much but take a description of the missing item in case it turned up for sale someday. Your buckle could, too."

"Maybe so. I thought of that myself."

Just then the kitchen phone rang. His grandmother went to answer it, and instead of talking at length as she usually did, she returned very soon. In a whisper she said, "It's Jay calling you!"

Paul was shocked. "What does he want?"

"He wants you to come over to his house right away. He says he's got a wild idea and needs to talk to you. He talked to the Old One about you and Frank Hart last night, and she got mighty upset when she heard him say 'Frank Hart.' "

"Please tell him I'm not coming. Say I'm sick or whatever you want to say."

She sat down across from him. *"No! Think!* Would Jay take a silver teapot and vases and a box? No, he wouldn't. And if he called you to come over to his home, would he steal from you? I'd bet he wouldn't; thieves aren't eager to see people they've stolen from. Paul, the Old One recognized Frank Hart's name. Aren't you curious about that? I am. Go talk to Jay."

Paul reflected on what his grandmother had said. Maybe

she was right; at least he should hear what the boy had to say. He went to the phone and said curtly, "Okay, I got your message, Jay. I'll bike on over, but it better be worth the ride."

Jay's voice sounded excited. "I think it's going to be. Come over right now. The Old One's awake."

After Paul finished eating, he got onto the borrowed bike and pedaled the twelve blocks to Jay's house.

It was a small, old brown cottage sandwiched between two taller houses. Jay met Paul on the front porch and cried out, "Come on in. She's still awake. She sleeps a lot of the time. Mom's gone to work but Lewis is coming over. I called him and asked him to come over and help us."

Trying not to show the suspicion he still felt toward Jay, Paul parked his bicycle and went inside the dimly lit little living room. A tiny, dried-up old lady in a pink bathrobe sat in a big overstuffed chair next to the fireplace. Even though it was June, a fire was burning in it. The old woman's hair was pure white, her deeply wrinkled face was dark brown, and her hands like animal paws.

Jay spoke loudly to the old woman, "This is my friend, Paul."

Friend? The word made Paul want to snort, but he didn't.

Jay went on. "Paul has a letter signed by Frank Hart."

Had would be a better word, thought Paul.

At the name "Frank Hart," the woman started in her

chair. She looked at Paul with sharp black eyes, and all at once she began to speak. He couldn't understand a word she was saying.

Jay told him, "She's talking in Ute. She goes too fast for me. I can't get what she says very well. Lewis will be able to. He lived on the reservation longer than I did, and he's studying languages at college. Hey, here he is now."

Paul looked behind him and saw a slight, casually dressed Indian man noiselessly entering the house. In his late twenties, Lewis Scarfe had the same black hair and deep-toned skin as Jay's. When the Indian boy introduced him, Scarfe gripped Paul's hand so hard it hurt. Then he turned to Jay and said, "She's talking, huh? Must be the first time in a month. What set her off this time?"

"The name 'Frank Hart.' It started her off last night and it's done the same thing again. She used some English words last night. It's all Ute now."

"Well, let's listen to what she has to say."

Lewis took a chair near the old woman, and the two boys sat on hassocks to listen to the flow of words. Lewis translated as she spoke.

"She just said 'bad men' and 'red rocks'," he said, and spoke to her in Ute.

Paul saw her nod and go on excitedly. Lewis listened again, then told the boys, "A lot of what she's saying is about Chief Ouray and his wife, Chipeta, and that the Old One's related to her. It's all mixed up, though. She said

'black place' just now, and 'dead men.' And did you hear
her say 'Indian Peaks' in English?"

"No," answered Jay. "It came too fast for me, Lewis."

Paul said, "Ask her about Frank Hart, please."

The Old One had heard Paul. She hissed clearly, "Frank
Hart, *kah-chi, kai-yah!*" and then a torrent of other words in
Ute. Eventually, the old woman began to rock to and fro as
she talked.

All the while, Scarfe listened intently, nodding. After a
time he turned to the boys and said, "I don't get this. She
just now talked about 'rocks dancing' and 'long time back,'
and four times in a row she's said 'red boy.' "

Jay asked, "Does she mean other Indians?"

"No, I don't think so. She'd use special words if she
meant that. All she means, I think, is 'red' and 'boy.' 'Kah-
chi, kai-yah' means 'bad.' This doesn't make sense, Jay.
She's just babbling now. I've got to get back to my thesis.
I'll see you later. Nice meeting you, Paul." And Lewis was
gone.

The moment the screen door closed behind him, the old
woman reached out and grabbed Paul, who sat nearest her,
by the forearm. With the other hand she pointed at him.
From her lips came one English word, "bus." She said it
again. "Bus." Then she hissed, "Frank Hart," and spoke
three words in Ute. After this, she sat back and closed her
eyes.

"Paul." Jay's voice was low and vibrant. "She just said

105

'red boy' again. I know those words. She said, 'Frank Hart is red boy.' "

Paul's mind raced. He asked, "Is she saying that he was an Indian? But your friend Lewis said she would use other words to talk about Indians."

"Yes, she would. I know those words. I think maybe she's saying that Frank Hart is Kid Ruby. Remember, she said 'red rocks.' They could mean rubies as well as rocks that are red colored."

"Yeah, rubies." Paul's face darkened. "You mean my buckle, huh?"

"Yes, if she ever saw rubies, she might not know the name for them. She'd probably say 'red rocks.' And 'bus' could be the stagecoach that never came. She calls anything that has wheels on it a bus. Paul, I've been thinking a lot since yesterday. Look at this." Shaking with excitement, Jay now reached into his shirt pocket and took out a purple-colored light bulb.

"What's that?"

"Something to show up secret writing. In the last century, they used to do it with lemon juice or sugar and water or blood. I don't have to mow any lawns today. Let's go over to your house and look at the Frank Hart letter with this. I got the idea when I studied my copy last night. I should have asked you to bring the letter over but I got so excited this morning I forgot. I want to look at all that empty space on the left side of the letter opposite the heart. We'll hold the letter under this light, and if that doesn't work we can warm the paper up or use iodine on it to see if there's any secret writing. If Frank Hart used lemon juice, it will come out if the paper is heated up. If it's blood, iodine will make it come out. The blue light can bring out other liquids that could have been used."

Paul Braun sat as if glued to his hassock. Jay *wasn't* the thief! Someone else—maybe the thief who had burglarized the whole neighborhood—took the buckle and letter.

Anger burned in Paul against the thief as he told the other boy in a harsh voice, "There's no use going over to my house. You can't look at the real letter, Jay. Somebody swiped it last night while we were gone and took the belt buckle, too. I think the thief was really after the buckle and just took the letter because the buckle was on top of it. He might have just scooped up both of them together."

Jay spoke so angrily and loudly that the Old One jerked awake. "No! I need to see the letter." The Ute boy's fury removed all doubt from Paul that he could have taken the buckle and letter, and he felt ashamed at having ever suspected his new friend. "Who took it?" demanded Jay.

"I don't know. Things got ripped off all over Grandmother's neighborhood last night. She didn't call the police about the buckle because it isn't worth much."

"How did the burglar get inside her house?"

"Up a ladder to my room. I left the window open."

"Did you look around the ladder for clues, Paul? Footprints, maybe?"

"Nope."

Jay was scowling. "Well, you're sure no detective! A good detective would have looked. Let's go over there right now and find out what we can. My ancestors were pretty good trackers. Maybe this twentieth-century Indian is, too."

As Jay grinned at his joke, a new thought struck Paul. If there *was* secret writing on the letter, maybe that was what the thief was after, not the buckle at all. Would the secret writing solve the Frank Hart–Billy Smart–Kid Ruby mystery?

8

A
RENDEZVOUS

At the Weber house Paul and Jay carefully examined the soil around the base of the ladder. Because the weather had been dry, the bare ground was very hard. Though some pansies had been trampled, there were no footprints or traces of shoe marks to be seen.

Then, while Paul's grandmother stood below, the boys went up the ladder one after the other. They looked on each rung and on the windowsill for fibers from clothing but found only some green fuzz that Mrs. Weber said came from an old sweater she wore gardening.

Once inside Paul's room, Jay asked if anything had been disturbed on the bureau top or messed up in the drawers.

At Paul's reply, "No, Jay," the Ute boy sat down on the bed, looking discouraged.

Paul sat down beside him and said, "I've been trying to think of all the people who might have known where I kept the buckle when I wasn't wearing it. There's Kelly and Brian and her dad and also Matthew Smart, the librarian."

Sounding surprised, Jay asked, "How did he know that?"

"I saw him last night at his mom's house. He asked me about the buckle, and I told him I'd left it home in my room. After that, he left the party. The rest of us stayed till after ten."

Jay nodded. "Did he like the buckle?"

"He seemed to. I don't know. He thought it was kind of loud but he knew it had real rubies."

"Could he have come here and grabbed the buckle and the letter?"

"He had lots of time to after he left. Jay, what about the Morses and Brian?" Paul snapped his fingers. "Let's go visit Mr. Morse right now. We'll tell him a dirty robber stole the buckle and watch his face. He could look guilty."

"Maybe not."

"But it's worth a try. We'll wait until we see Kelly go there. She and Brian usually do around noontime. If we're lucky we can catch all three of them at the same time. We can tell them that the police have a description of the thief who committed all the other robberies around here. That could scare them if one of them did it."

"It's an idea, I guess. Mr. Morse could have taken the

110

other stuff, too, just to throw everyone off. We've got some time before noon. What do you think of what the Old One said this morning?"

"That was a lot of stuff to take in all at once. By the way, what does Lewis Scarfe know about the buckle and the letter?"

"I told him a little about them. He's awful busy at school and with his karate lessons. He didn't listen much. I don't think he really heard me till I told him about the old stagecoach. He's a Ute and knows that the old Utes were suspected of attacking it. That got to him and he listened when I said I wanted to write up the old story. He even said he'd try to help me."

"Jay, are you sure he wouldn't have come here after my buckle?"

"I don't think he would, though he was interested when he heard it was ruby studded. I didn't tell him that I thought there might be secret ink on the Frank Hart letter. He said he never heard of Frank Hart or Kid Ruby—only the stagecoach. Paul, have you got a pencil and paper? I want to write down what the Old One said before I forget it. I can't count on her coming up with anything again. She'll sleep for hours now. She always does when she gets real tired or upset."

"Is it okay to leave her alone?"

"Yes, she can get up by herself and go to bed or the bathroom. There's an old neighbor woman who looks in on her during the day."

Paul got up, got a pencil, and ripped a sheet of paper from the tablet he was using to write down facts of Billy Smart's career.

As he wrote on his knee, Jay spoke aloud. " 'Bad men.' That could mean soldiers to her, or outlaws, or even the Indians who hated us Utes. 'Red rocks' could mean the rubies that are a red color or just red-colored rocks. 'Black place'—that could mean a lot of things that are dark. 'Red boy,' I'm sure, doesn't mean an Indian kid. Since she said it when she got upset at the name of Frank Hart, I think that she means Kid Ruby. She said 'dancing rocks' and that doesn't make any sense at all. 'Bus' could mean stagecoach or it could mean she wanted to go for a ride in Mom's car. What else did she say?"

" 'Dead men.' Remember, that's what Lewis said she said."

"Yes, that could mean everybody she knows has been dead a long time or it could mean that Frank Hart or Kid Ruby are dead. Or it could be the people on the coach." Jay put the pencil down. "That's all she said that I remember."

"No, it isn't! You and I didn't catch it, but Lewis did. He said she said 'Indian Peaks' in English. Where's that?"

"Not far from here. It's in a pass between here and Fairplay." Jay stood up suddenly, his dark eyes shining. "Paul, that's on the road the old coach took!"

Near noon the boys got on their bikes and went to Morse's jewelry store in the shopping mall. As they had

112

figured, Mr. Morse, Kelly, and Brian were there, eating take-out hamburger lunches. In the back behind the glass partition, Paul could see Mr. Dobbs eating a sandwich.

Kelly hailed Paul and Jay, but neither boy responded to her greeting.

Her father told Paul, "You look like you just ate a sour pickle."

Brian added, "No, a hot green chili pepper."

Paul told them, "I don't feel so good. Somebody came to my neighborhood last night and robbed some houses when the people were away from home. He hit our house, too, and swiped my belt buckle. The police have an idea who did it, though."

"Oh, no!" Kelly plunked down her soda on the counter while Brian stopped his halfway to his mouth.

Paul observed them carefully. Their surprise and shock seemed very real to him and he stopped suspecting them. Mr. Morse said heavily, "That's rotten luck, son. It was an interesting old piece. This store was hit last year, and the same thing happened in my neighborhood. Some power tools of mine were stolen out of my garage last spring."

Kelly said, "Somebody took my bike from out in front of my school. They lifted it up, chain, lock, and all, and took it."

Mr. Dobbs came slowly from the rear of the shop. He said, "Thieves took over a thousand dollars in gold ladies' neck chains from here. They were insured, but a diamond-set wristwatch I was repairing wasn't. I'd let my insurance policy lapse. I lost nine hundred dollars on that crime." He shook his head. "I don't repair diamond-studded items anymore. I don't care to carry that much insurance."

Jay asked, "And the gold neck chains never showed up again?"

"No, they never did," said Mr. Morse. "They were sold in some thieves' market somewhere, I imagine." He turned to Paul, "What else was taken from your grandmother's house?"

"Nothing from hers, but an old silver teapot and a box and a couple of old Chinese vases were taken from the other houses."

"All antique articles," said Mr. Morse. "They knew what they were after, then. Usually burglars want transistor radios and cameras and TV sets and stereo systems. What kind of description do the police have?"

Paul said quickly, "They didn't tell me. One of the neighbors must have got a look at him. Grandma and I were out to dinner when my buckle and that old letter Frank Hart wrote were stolen."

Brian Holmes exclaimed, "What—somebody took that old letter, too?"

"Yeah."

"That's crazy," came from Kelly.

Paul explained, "The letter and the buckle were together."

Kelly said sadly, "You got to like it a lot, didn't you?"

"Yes. At first I didn't, but after a while I did."

"We all liked it," said her father. "There was something about it, even for me—and by now I've seen a lot of antique jewelry. It was unique. I doubt if there's another in the world like it. It's a pity you lost it, Paul. There was real old-time craftsmanship in it."

Trying to be polite and not show how much the loss upset him, Paul now asked Kelly, "How are you doing on your research?"

"Okay, I guess. I went to the downtown library this morning. I'm reading up on Dr. Florence Rena Sabin now. She was a college professor who was born just about the same time Billy Smart was, so that makes her a pioneer." The girl laughed and added, "Brian's doing great on the old mines and miners. He's found an old poem he's fallen in love with."

Brian corrected her, "It's not a poem. It's a song. I memorized it even if I don't know the tune. This is how it goes:

"My sweetheart's a mule in the mines
I drive her all day without lines
   On the car front I sit
   And tobacco I spit
All over my sweetheart's behind."

Mr. Morse laughed and told the four of them, "I haven't heard that since I was a little kid. Long ago, miners used mules to pull the ore cars in the old mines. They use me-

115

chanical cars these days. Keeping the mules underground for weeks at a time would definitely come under the heading of cruelty to animals today. Life was a lot tougher in the last century—for men and women as well as for animals."

Paul told him, "I'm glad they don't use mules for that work anymore." He nudged Jay and said, "We better go now, huh."

"Okay, Paul."

When they were out on the mall some minutes later, Paul asked, "Jay, what do you think? Did one of them take the buckle and the letter?"

"I dunno. If one of them wasn't surprised to hear what you said, he—or she—was sure a good actor."

"Yes, but maybe they—I mean, whoever did it—thought I'd come by, and was ready to act a part. Jay, you didn't say anything about secret ink on the letter."

"No, and neither did you. That was good. If one of 'em has the letter, why let 'em know that we think something could be on the left side of it."

Paul said, "I guess we have to keep Kelly in mind, too."

"Sure, we do. She could climb up a ladder as good as anybody else could. Paul, can you find out where Matthew Smart lives and when he won't be at home?"

"I think I can."

"Okay, find out today. Meet me after dark outside your house without your grandmother knowing about it. We'll go to Smart's house and take a look around. Are you game to do that, Paul?"

116

Paul swallowed hard, then said, "What if we find the buckle and the letter? What'll we do?"

"Take 'em back. That won't be stealing. We won't take anything that belongs to Smart. Wear dark clothes. I'll bring stuff for our faces and hands."

"What kind of stuff?"

"Grease. Black grease, the kind commandos use—and Indian braves used on the warpath, Paleface Paul!"

Though he had misgivings about the coming night's event and felt strange sensations in his stomach, Paul made up his mind to do what Jay had suggested. He wanted his buckle back. Maybe the librarian who had been so pleasant had taken it. But that was hard to believe—who had ever heard of a crook librarian? It didn't bother Paul that Jay was almost giving him orders at times. After all, Jay knew the state and the town and he, Paul, a stranger from the East Coast, was glad to have such a friend helping him. By now he was utterly sure that Jay had not taken the buckle or letter. If he had, Jay would want to avoid his company, and it would be easy for him to, with his lawn mowing and yard-work jobs.

While his grandmother was out weeding her petunias, Paul called the library and learned Matthew Smart's hours for that day. Smart would be working until nine. After finding his address in Mrs. Weber's address book, Paul looked on a street map and saw it wasn't too far from the Weber house.

At seven Paul told Mrs. Weber that he wanted to go up to his room and read more on Buffalo Bill. At eight he dressed in his darkest clothing and went out the window and down the ladder. Jay was there at the bottom. He gave Paul a jar from which both boys smeared their faces with black grease. Then they hurried away on foot, loping down the dark streets, and in ten minutes' time arrived at the small gray house where Matthew Smart lived. One light burned inside.

Paul and Jay circled the house, listening for a dog's bark or any other sounds inside, but heard none. Jay tried the windows until he found one that was unlocked. He and Paul opened it, then crawled inside onto a back porch. Jay had a little flashlight with him and switched it on.

The two boys now went through the rooms from kitchen to dinette to living room to bathroom, and finally to the bedroom. This was where the buckle and letter would probably be. They began looking—Paul searching the two bureaus, Jay going through the pockets of all the clothing hanging in the closet. They looked in boxes under the bed, under the mattress and pillows, in vases and in the bookshelf behind books. Everywhere! But the only buckles they found were those permanently attached to Smart's belts.

Finally Paul whispered, "The buckle isn't in this room— the letter isn't either, and we don't have time to look for the letter in his study. It'll be full of papers the way my step-dad's study is. Jay, we better get out of here *now*. Look at that clock beside his bed. It's five minutes to nine!"

118

The boys left the way they had come, going out the back window and carefully shutting it again. Though they had worked fast, they had disturbed nothing in the bedroom to alert Smart's suspicions. They were starting alongside the house to reach the front when their luck ran out. A car was entering the driveway. *Smart!*

"He's too soon," whispered Jay, looking at his wristwatch, "and his clock's wrong. Let's get out of here—fast."

As they hurried out behind the house, they saw the headlights of the car as it came up the driveway that led to the garage in the back.

"Paul!" hissed Jay, pointing to a tall cherry tree on the far side of the yard.

The boys raced to it and leaped up, grabbing hold of some low branches and hurriedly climbing into the tree. There they sat on a limb behind a thick growth of leaves. Paul's heart thudded as he saw Matthew Smart get out of a dark-colored car, and it raced even faster when he spied a big German shepherd dog climb out of it, too. While Smart unlocked the garage door to put his car inside, the dog began to nose about the yard. It stopped at the base of the boys' tree and sniffed at it. Then it stood up on its hind legs and began to bark.

"Prinz," came Smart's shout. "Get over here. You just got out of the animal hospital a half hour ago. Your smeller's off from being there. It's only that old opossum that's always lived in the cherry tree. Come on inside and I'll feed you. *Food,* Prinz, *food*!"

To Paul's relief the word "food" got the dog away and into the house. Paul asked Jay, "How long do you think we have to stay up here?"

"Till Smart locks up the back and turns off the back porch and kitchen lights."

Paul said, "I don't think we'll ever know if he took my buckle or not."

"Yeah, Paul, you're probably right. I'm glad we didn't have to explain what we're doing up in his cherry tree wearing black grease."

"*You're glad!* My grandmother's a friend of the Smart family. I hate to think what she'd have to say if she found out I sneaked out and searched Matthew Smart's house. I don't think I want to do anymore detecting."

Jay muttered, "I think we just ran out of people to detect on."

Fifteen minutes later the lights went out in the back of the house and on in front, so the boys got down out of the tree. A block away they wiped their faces with the tissues Jay had brought.

Before separating to go to their own homes, they decided to rendezvous the next morning at Mrs. Weber's house and tell her what they'd learned from the Old One that morning. Perhaps Paul's grandmother might be able to help when she heard the list of words Jay had written down. After all, three heads were better than two!

Paul got back up the ladder and into his room without being discovered. He locked the window after him, undressed, and got into bed, but he could not sleep. So much had happened today to keep him awake. He looked at the little clock beside his bed. Its dial glowed in the dark. Paul saw it reach eleven, and ten minutes afterward he heard the musical sound of his grandmother's boudoir clock strike the hour in her room. It was off ten minutes. It had been losing more and more time each day, and its inaccuracy had begun to irritate her. At supper that night she'd complained about it again. She didn't want to get rid of it, though, because it had been a Christmas gift from Lance and she valued it for sentimental reasons.

Thinking about the old clock made Paul think of Bronco Billy Smart's buckle. By now the boy felt almost as if Billy Smart himself had given it to him. It was a gaudy gift and of little worth today; yet Paul valued it for sentimental reasons, as his grandmother valued Lance's Christmas clock.

The more he read about old Billy, the more real—and sad—the old-time cowboy star became. Billy had never married. There were no children, grandchildren, or great-grandchildren to love and remember him. He'd traveled around much of his life, and, though famous, he belonged nowhere and to nobody. He had left behind only a few possessions, and now two of them had been stolen by a thief. And it was all his, Paul's, fault—he had worn the buckle and attracted attention by bragging about it. Grandma Weber should have kept it! By losing it, he'd hurt her.

Well, if he could, he intended to spend the rest of the summer trying to get it back for her—and for Billy, too.

121

9

AN
ATTACK

When Paul came down the next morning he saw the bedroom clock on the kitchen table. Mrs. Weber waved toward it and said, "It's got to go to Mr. Morse's shop for repair today before it drives me up the wall." She laughed as she broke eggs in a skillet. "I almost married Pete Dobbs's father back during World War Two, but your grandfather came along and I married him instead. The Dobbs I liked became a flier after the war. He was crazy about airplanes. He married a high school classmate of mine. They were both killed in a crash in a cross-country air race when their son was just entering his teens. They're an old family here."

Paul said, "Yeah, I remember you said they were. So is Kelly's family. Grandma, Jay's coming over this morning to talk to you. We've found out some new things, and we want to know what you think."

Sally Weber looked at Paul. "Well, I'm flattered! What about Jay's summer jobs?"

"He postponed 'em."

"Too bad you can't postpone grass growing. All right, when he comes I'll listen. Then the clock goes to the shop."

Jay came at nine-thirty and went into the living room with Paul. Mrs. Weber was at her needlepoint frame. She stitched away, poking the needle through the stiff canvas as she listened again to the two boys repeating what they had learned about Kid Ruby in the microfilmed papers, and of his possibly being Frank Hart.

Finally she said, "So, you think Bronco Billy's father was the outlaw, Kid Ruby? I never heard of him."

Jay said, "Yes, but I don't think he was an outlaw for long."

"You mean he 'reformed'?"

"I don't know, Mrs. Weber. It's just that the papers stopped talking about him. There's more, though—what we learned yesterday from the Old One at my house." Now Jay took the piece of paper with the list of words and read them aloud to her. She stopped sewing and repeated, "red boy," "dead men," "bus." At "bus" she frowned deeply and said, "That's an odd word in that list."

"We think so, too."

Paul asked, "Do you know what 'dancing rocks' and 'black place' mean?"

"No, I have no idea at all. Do you, Jay?"

"Not really. I talked to Lewis Scarfe on the way over here. He's the translator for the Old One. He doesn't know what they mean either."

"It's all most mysterious and exciting, isn't it?" She turned to Paul. "I don't know how all this fits together. Probably it doesn't fit. But it's fascinating to wonder if Kid Ruby is Frank Hart and if Frank Hart is Bronco Billy's father. If so, no wonder he took the name Smart. It wouldn't have been healthy for him to be known as the offspring of an outlaw. People didn't think that romantic in the old days. They would have been waiting for Billy to turn bad, too."

"Grandmother, the Old One also said the words 'Indian Peaks.' Jay says it's a real place. It's on the old stagecoach route between here and Fairplay."

Mrs. Weber smiled. "I know that road well. It's been a long time since I was on it, though. It's not far from here. If you want, we can go up there today. I'm free. I'll fix a picnic lunch and after we drop off my clock, we'll drive there to eat. Could you come, Jay? We would like to have you with us."

"Sure, thanks." Jay smiled.

"Good. I have time to fry some chicken and make some salad. We'll leave at eleven-thirty. We can find a ravine off the road in the Indian Peaks area where we can eat our lunch. It's a beautiful summer day for an outing. It'll do me good to get out; and you, Paul, should have been doing some sightseeing before this. Jay, maybe you'll get some hunches about your coach by being close to where it disappeared. Let's forget about the stolen buckle now—it's gone. We won't see it again. Paul, you wore it in family pride for a while! That's enough for me. Let's make this a day for all of us to remember fondly."

Paul smiled, glad to hear that his grandmother wasn't feeling too sad about the buckle being gone.

Now she asked Jay, "Should you call somebody to let them know where you're going?"

"I'll call my mom where she works. She won't mind if I come with you so long as I get home before dark."

"Tell her you certainly will."

At eleven thirty-five Mrs. Weber was ready with the picnic hamper. Paul and Jay had helped get the lunch ready, making sandwiches and a green salad. As they worked, Sally Weber had told them, "A boy's place is in the kitchen as much as a girl's is in the workshop. By the time you leave here, Paul, you'll know a thing or two about cooking for yourself. If I could learn to fix fuses and use a hammer and hatchet and saw at fifty—just a few years ago—you can learn how to fry a chicken or roast a piece of beef at thirteen. Later on, you'll thank me, and so will your wife."

"Wife?" This had made both boys grin. Paul didn't mind, though. It would be fun to surprise his mother and

Jesse with something he had cooked when he went home.

Before they left, though, Paul's grandmother phoned Mrs. Smart to thank her for the superb dinner she and Paul had been invited to. Paul heard her tell Mrs. Smart that they were off to Indian Peaks to picnic that afternoon.

After his grandmother hung up, Paul toted the hamper to the old green car while Jay carried mats and blankets to sit on. Mrs. Weber carefully brought out her clock in a cardboard box and set it on the front seat beside her while the two boys climbed into the back. Then she drove to the mall and parked, leaving them to wait inside the car. She went into Mr. Morse's store with the box, and Paul could see her talking to both Morse and Dobbs. At one point, Sally Weber gestured toward the car and the boys. Then she came back, slid behind the wheel, and headed out of town.

As she drove, she told them, "There's no rush getting there. Let's go through some parts of the city Paul hasn't seen yet. Maybe next week we'll go see the Garden of the Gods rock formations and the Broadmoor Hotel. They're famous here in the Springs."

Jay asked Paul, "Have you seen the Air Force Academy yet?"

Before her grandson could answer, Mrs. Weber replied, "No, he hasn't; but he will before he goes home. He has to see its famous chapel. It's a marvel of architecture." She chuckled. "And its *not* Colonial! George Washington didn't worship there. In fact, it would astonish him."

Paul stifled a groan. His grandmother stuck a spear in Delaware every so often. She didn't need to. He liked Colorado just fine. It was exciting here.

Some thirty minutes after they had left the outskirts of the town they were climbing into mountain country, heading west. Mrs. Weber explained to Paul, "We go through a pass. It's supposed to be solid granite cliffs."

Jay said solemnly, "That's what's so funny about the old coach disappearing. It happened in a pass where there were rock walls on each side and no through roads going away from the road."

"Yes, this is rock walls and some narrow shallow ravines that dead-end in sheer rock," agreed Mrs. Weber. "I used to hike in the area as a girl scout. There were some Indian picture writings, as I recall. We went in and out of a number of ravines. You couldn't get lost in them if you tried to."

Jay spoke softly, almost to himself. "I heard about the picture writing up here. They're old Ute petroglyphs." Paul waited for the Ute boy to go on, but that was all he said.

On and on they went, for thirty miles, until high cliffs of dark rock loomed over them to the left and right. Trees grew from out of the cliffs and on top of them. The pass was a gloomy place, a "black place," as the Old One had said, with very dark gray rocks all around them. Paul was glad when Mrs. Weber said they were nearing the end of

127

the pass and that she would pull off into one of the ravines for their picnic.

Suddenly, a dark-colored new model sedan came around a curve from behind them and hurtled past at high speed. It went by so swiftly that Paul didn't get a real look at the driver. All he saw was the dark shape of a head and a torso hunched over the wheel as the driver raced by them.

Mrs. Weber yelped, "Who was that madman? He's got to be drunk or crazy! Did either one of you get his license number?"

Jay was leaning forward with his fists clenched, staring intently ahead. He said, "Nobody could have! He went by too fast."

Sally Weber muttered, "I'm not going to try to catch up with him so we can find out the number. The ravine I recall is only a mile or so ahead, around the next bend in the road."

When her car made that turn a few minutes later, the three received their second unpleasant surprise of the trip. The car that had sped by them so recklessly was parked across the left-hand side of the narrow road, blocking both lanes. There was no way to pass it.

"What in the world?" cried Mrs. Weber, braking her car to avoid hitting the other one.

As she came to a stop, the door on the driver's side of the dark brown sedan opened and a man got out. He had on a navy blue jumpsuit that covered his clothes. On his head he wore a knitted, black ski mask that had holes for eyes, nose, and mouth. Over one shoulder he carried coiled ropes, and in his right hand was a blue-metal pistol, which he pointed directly at them.

In a grating falsetto voice he called out, "Park here and get out of the car fast, all of you. I know what you're up to!"

Keeping her nerve, Mrs. Weber told the boys, "Please, do what he tells us. Don't ever argue with a gun."

Paul asked her quietly, "What does he think we're up to?"

"I don't know. You two, get out of the car and stand beside me."

She parked the car and all three got out to stand with their hands in the air.

The masked man came slowly up to them and said, "Turn around and move off ahead of me back down the road. I'll tell you where to stop. Now, *go!*"

Paul, his grandmother, and Jay walked in a line ahead of the man until he ordered, "Go down that gully to the left."

Mrs. Weber told him, "I've got thirty dollars in my wallet. That's all. Take it and leave us alone."

"I don't want your money," the man answered still in the falsetto voice. "I've already got what I needed from you. Now you three get down there."

The ravine was narrow and rock-filled. Throwing down three of his ropes, the man motioned with the pistol and or-

129

dered, "You, the Indian kid, tie up the woman first. *Tight.*"

When Jay had finished, Paul was ordered to tie Jay. He did so with shaking fingers. Then he tied his own feet. When he'd finished, his attacker set his pistol atop a big rock, and rolled Paul over roughly. After securing the boy's wrists, he retrieved his pistol.

His work done, the man left them, climbing out of the ravine with the last coil of rope over his shoulder.

Once he was out of sight, Mrs. Weber was first to speak. Her voice shaking, she said, "We'll be all right, boys. Our car'll be spotted sooner or later by the highway patrol. They'll come looking for us. They're going to find a full picnic hamper inside the car, and that'll make them wonder about us. It could take hours, though, before they find us. I think we're lucky he didn't shoot us."

Jay's voice didn't waver as he told her, "He's got better things to do. He didn't plan to shoot us, just get rid of us. I think he knows you, Mrs. Weber. Did you hear him say he didn't want your money, and that he'd got something from you that he wanted?"

Paul said softly, "Yes, the ruby buckle."

"No, the old letter, even though he took them both."

Mrs. Weber put in, "It's somebody who *knows* me. Who could that be?"

Paul felt that he knew and told her angrily, "Mr. Morse or Mr. Smart. They both know you and could know where we were going today. But why should they get so mad that we're going on a picnic? That's all we're up to. If Matthew Smart had called his mother this morning, she could have mentioned where we were going. He could have driven out here real fast. He's got a dark-colored car." Then, turning to Jay, he added, "It could even be Lewis Scarfe, you know."

Jay made a sound of protest, but Paul told him, "Don't be so sure about Lewis. He's the right size and build."

Jay replied, "Yes, any one of those three could be this guy. They're all the same build. You should have left some slack in my rope, Paul. Can you move your hands at all?"

Paul pushed with all his strength against his bonds. Yes, the ropes tying his wrists gave a little bit. He said, "Mine aren't that tight."

"Good," said Jay. "I'm going to roll over next to you. Put your hands where I tell you so I can use my teeth on your ropes. Let's just hope I can do it."

Jay rolled over to him and Paul lay still, feeling movement at his wrists and hearing the sound of panting and spitting. Finally Jay ordered, "Try to wiggle your hands."

Paul did, and felt the ropes loosening. A minute more of Jay biting at the knots and spitting out hemp fibers and the rope came free.

It took Paul only a short while to free his ankles. Then he untied his grandmother, and with her help made quick work of freeing Jay.

Mrs. Weber looked at her wristwatch. "We left the car

forty-five minutes ago. Let's go back to it. I'm sure who-ever did this has driven off by now. Did either of you get his license number as we walked past his car?"

Paul told her, "He was parked sideways to us and we never got near it."

She sighed. "Well, he gave us a bad time, but we're all right. We'll go back to the main road and alert the highway patrol. The car was a 1983 Buick. I know that much. A friend of mine has one like it but in a different color. Come on, let's go."

The three of them trudged back to the road and down to where the green car was parked. The dark Buick was there, too. It was empty, but locked and now parked along the shoulder. The Weber car was unlocked but the car keys were missing.

"We can't leave!" Mrs. Weber cried in frustration. "We're going to have to wait here for somebody to come along to help us. I just hope it won't be the man with the mask."

In the meantime Paul had gone up to the Buick and memorized the license number. Returning to the others he said, "Let's walk back toward town."

"*No, Paul!*" Jay's voice was firm. He added, "That guy won't be back here for a while. I'm sure of that. Get both flashlights out of your grandmother's car and come along with me."

"Jay, what do you plan to do?" asked Mrs. Weber.

"Go exploring, right now. Look in the ravine just ahead

of us, the one with the dead tree over on that cliff. I've heard about that tree. We're going to go looking in there for the picture rock."

She asked, "You mean the petroglyphs?"

"Yes. We want to find the sun and a snake on a big rock. The Old One called me to her bed last night and told me. My mom was going to take me—and you, too, Paul—out here on Saturday afternoon, but then your grandmother said we'd be coming today. I didn't tell you earlier this morning because I wanted to surprise you when we got here. The Old One drew me a picture of the sun with rays coming out of it and a wavy snake. Then she said 'black rock' and 'dancing rock' again in Ute, and moved her hand around while she was saying 'dancing rock.' She sort of made a circle. I think it's a rock that can move."

"Swivels?" asked Mrs. Weber.

Jay nodded coolly. "Could be. I think the rock blocks the entrance to a cave. That would be her 'black place.' Then she said 'bus' again. I think she *was* talking about the old stagecoach. It could be inside there!"

Paul felt the thrill start at the soles of his feet and go all the way to the roots of his hair. He gave one of the flashlights to Jay and looked at his grandmother. Her face was white. Then she and Paul started after Jay.

As they walked, Sally Weber told Jay, "If it is there and the Utes knew, then they must have attacked the stage. Do you want to find that out?"

"I thought of that, and I thought of the gold, too. Yes, I

133

still want to know—no matter what we find."

"Jay, what if this is the cave the man in the mask is looking for?"

"I don't think so."

"But how can you be sure?" Paul asked. "If he's got the letter and there is secret writing on it, that might tell about getting into the cave with a rope."

Jay told him, "The secret writing can't be telling about the 'dancing rock' that swivels. He wouldn't need a rope to get in that way. We don't know where he went, but it must be to some other cave. There are lots of stories of lost gold in this part of the state, and lots of caves here. The letter probably told about one of them. Say, we'd better stop talking. If he's nearby we don't want him to hear us."

They walked in silence until Jay motioned them to stop. Leaving the road swiftly, he plunged into a wide ravine, over which hung a long-dead tree with a distinct eagle's-nest bulge at its top.

As Mrs. Weber stood waiting beside Paul she said, "We shouldn't be taking the time to do this. We should stay with the car in case someone comes along."

"But, Grandma, that dude could come back. If he finds us untied he could shoot us or something. We're safer out of sight down here. Let's do what Jay wants—for a little while anyhow."

The Ute boy came back as fast as he had gone, and now motioned for them to follow him. Some hundreds of feet farther into the ravine he gestured for them to wait and went on ahead again. It was a longer wait this time. Finally Jay returned, beckoning wildly.

"It's there! I found 'em! The sun and the snake! They're hard to see, and high up, but they're there. There's a sort of broad path lower down that leads right to 'em. Be careful how you walk, Mrs. Weber, the ground's not even."

"Don't worry about me, Jay."

The three carefully picked their way down to a large protruding rock. Paul saw that it had faint carvings on it. He could just about make out a rayed sun and a long, wavy snakelike line. But the rock was enormous. Who could move it? No, this could not be a "dancing rock."

He told Jay, "It's like you say here, but what'll we do about this gigantic rock? It'd take a herd of elephants to move it."

"No, I don't think so. If we all push together right here"— and he pointed to an Indian symbol carved in the rock at shoulder height—"it might move."

Mrs. Weber said, "It could crash down on top of us."

"No, it ought to slide on its bottom, I think."

Now Paul said, "Well, we'll find out. Let's push."

The boys set their flashlights down and all three shoved with all their strength on Jay's order, "Push." At first the rock didn't move. Then, slowly, grindingly, it did, sending a shower of pebbles and dirt down on their heads. Gasping from the effort, they went on pushing and, little by little, the great rock swiveled aside.

A rush of ice-cold, musty-smelling air struck Paul in the

135

face, and he tilted his head away from the boulder to catch his breath. As he did so, he found himself looking into inky blackness.

He called to Jay, "It *is* a cave!"

"I know. I can see it, too. We can stop now. This is wide enough for us to get in. Bring the flashlights, Paul."

Paul retrieved the lights, giving one to Jay, and the three then slid past the rock into the slit of darkness.

Jay spoke softly, his voice echoing nevertheless. "Okay, let's go on. We'll leave the opening the way it is. I'll go first, then you come, Paul, and then you, Mrs. Weber. Turn your beam on, Paul."

As Paul Braun pressed the flashlight button, he stepped into line behind Jay. He walked gingerly, following the Ute boy. Was Jay as nervous and excited as he was? Paul wondered. If so, he couldn't tell it from Jay's manner.

The three of them went down what seemed to be a long, wide, black tunnel. Eventually Jay turned to the right following the curve of the tunnel walls. The flashlight's beam now revealed that they were out of the tunnel and in a huge cavern.

"Ah-h-h, my God!" The words escaped Mrs. Weber's lips. Paul found himself instinctively repeating them.

The coach!

The coach that never came!

It was here, in the middle of this huge cave. There was no mistaking it. Painted black, with red-colored wheels, it was bigger than a modern automobile, much longer than Paul had thought it would be.

"Let's go look at it," said Jay.

Breathing deeply now, Paul, Jay, and Mrs. Weber approached the coach. Standing on tiptoe, Paul peered through one of the side windows, flashing his light about. There was nothing inside but seats of rotting, moldering leather. The coach's leather sides, too, hung down in long strips of decay, and its shafts lay on the floor of the cavern.

Mrs. Weber asked hoarsely, "Can you see the money box, boys?"

Jay had been walking around to the other side and was now on his knees before the coach. "Yes, it's over here, but the money's gone. I'd say the lock's been shot off."

"But where are the passengers and guards?"

"I dunno, Mrs. Weber. I can't figure it out. Let's see what else we can find, though."

"I don't think I care to," came from Mrs. Weber.

Paul turned to her. "Grandma, as long as we're here, we ought to explore; and we ought to stick together, too."

"Oh, all right. I can see when I'm outnumbered."

"Let's see what's behind those rocks over there," Jay suggested. "We'll go slow and be careful, though."

Still awed by the sight of the old coach, the three moved off in silence. As the Indian boy had guessed, they did find something beyond the rocks at the end of the great cave— human skeletons in a jumbled heap of bones and ragged garments.

Fighting nausea, Paul said, "That'll be the people on the stage. I bet they were forced to get down out of it and walk over here. Then they were murdered."

Jay was on his knees peering at the bones. After a moment he said, "Most of 'em were shot in the head."

Paul asked, "Would Utes do that?"

"Maybe so, but it doesn't seem right for my people in those days." Jay sighed and got up. "Let's see what else is in here."

Mrs. Weber told them, "I've lost all my appetite for a picnic."

"Me, too," said Paul, "but I agree with Jay. Let's go on."

Beyond the jutting rocks the sides of the cavern narrowed, creating another tunnel. As he followed behind Jay, Paul grew uneasy.

The walls seemed to close in around him and the path grew even narrower as he continued walking. At one place he was forced to stoop, and he felt his shirt rip on a piece of sharp jagged stone.

Finally they came to the end of the tunnel and were able to stand erect. They were in a cave smaller than the one that held the stagecoach. Picture writing and symbols covered the far wall. But it was not the petroglyphs that held their attention. It was the man standing beside three old open wooden chests. Slung across his body was a canvas sack; instinctively Paul knew the sack was filled with gold. It didn't matter. The man was pointing his pistol at them.

10

A
SURPRISE

It was the man from the road, with his coil of rope gone and his ski mask off. With a gasp of shock Paul recognized him—Peter Dobbs, the watch repairman from the mall.

"Peter," cried Mrs. Weber, "it's you."

"Yes, Mrs. Weber, it's me." Dobbs's face twisted into a snarl of anger. "I heard you coming, so I waited for you. You found the coach and the bones, but you couldn't be satisfied with that, could you? No, you had to come nosing around some more. I wish you hadn't done that." His voice rose as he pointed to the canvas bag. "I've got the stage-coach gold, and you can see I've got the pistol, too."

"But, Peter!" cried Paul's grandmother.

"Don't 'but Peter' me, Mrs. Weber. You never thought

I was anything but dull old Pete, the watchmaker, did you? Your son, Lance, who got to live in a big fancy house, used to tease me at school about how crazy I was. Well, I'm *not* nuts, and I'll take the time to tell you why now that you're here. When you came to the shop today, you told me where you were headed for your little picnic. Well, I knew you'd eat but I knew, too, that you'd do some snooping around, and somehow just might have learned where to go. I'd had a mind to come here to Indian Peaks this afternoon in any event. It's my afternoon off. But when I found out you were coming here, too, I figured I'd better get here first. So I took off work early and caught up with you.

"Well, you know who I am and you know that I've found the gold. I just wish you'd had the sense to stay tied up. How'd you get in here anyway? Is there another way in?"

"Yes," said Jay defiantly.

"Good. I figured there had to be once I saw the stagecoach. I was going to search for it when I finished looking through these old money chests. That old letter didn't mention the entrance you folks used. It only told about a hole in the top."

Despite his fear, Paul cried out accusingly, *"You* stole my buckle and the letter!"

"You're right, kid. I took both of them, though it was really just the letter I wanted. I kept watch on your house. When I saw you leave the other night, I knew it was the break I'd been waiting for. I got the ladder and climbed in through an open second floor window."

Mrs. Weber said, "Peter, I can't believe this. Please put that gun down."

"No, ma'am, I don't intend to." Turning to Paul, Dobbs continued. "You see, when you said the name, 'Frank Hart,' I knew it. And I knew what your letter meant, too, when you asked Morse and me about it. I had to get my hands on it and examine it. Now all of you come over here and sit down on the floor by these empty trunks that old Frank and his gang used to store loot in."

"Gang?" asked Paul after he and the others had sat down beneath the petroglyphs.

"That's what I said. *Gang.*"

Jay muttered, "This was an old Ute cave. It was sacred to my people."

"So it was, but they don't seem to care about it, or even remember it anymore." Dobbs laughed strangely. "Maybe they forgot it on purpose because of what old Kid Ruby used it for?"

Paul asked, "Then Frank Hart *was* Kid Ruby?"

"Yes. You're a smart boy. I like you. I wish you hadn't gotten mixed up in all this. You come along from the East and stumble onto something that me and my family have been looking for for over a hundred years. All my life, and my father's life, too, we've looked for the gold that was on that old stagecoach. My great-grandfather—he knew Kid Ruby. When I was just a boy, even younger than you two kids, he told me about Francis Xavier Marion Hart— Frank Hart for short."

141

Mrs. Weber whispered to Paul beside her, "That's what the long entry in the old Bible said, the one that was scratched out. It isn't an ink blot after all. John Blake's name—Sophronia's second husband—was written in on top of it. Billy Smart must have been Frank Hart's son."

Dobbs had been listening carefully to her and nodded. "He was and he kept it quiet. But I've held it inside me for so long that I've got to let it out now. We Dobbses have been on the trail of this gold for a long, long time. One of my ancestors rode with Kid Ruby and got shot up bad by him during a fight. He knew he was dying and wanted to get revenge on Ruby. So he told his brother, my great-grandfather, about the gang's plans to rob the payroll coach that ran between the Springs and Fairplay. He said that Kid Ruby planned to hide the loot underground somewhere in the area of this pass. He hadn't been taken there yet himself because he was new to the gang, so he didn't know the exact location. My great-granddad always figured that Kid Ruby had pulled off the robbery and then left the Territory right afterward, because he dropped out of sight like a rock tossed into a lake. But he wondered if Ruby left the gold hidden to come back for later on.

"We Dobbses have kept what we knew to ourselves, and for years my family's dug around here for the gold. I started digging with my father when I was in grade school. We didn't know if 'underground' meant a cave. That's why I had to get hold of Frank Hart's letter. I'd guessed it might have secret writing when you showed it to Morse and me. I

142

spotted that big blank space on it then. I knew that old-timers used secret inks, so when I got hold of the letter, I held it close to a candle. Just as I figured, the heat brought out some writing. It described a big cave in this area with Indian markings on the front and a hole in the top near a tree. The letter must have gotten wet, because the rest of the secret writing was too blurred to read. I'd guessed that hole was going to be the way in, but the blurred part must have told about the way you came in. Anyway, I found the hole and shinnied down a rope for nearly fifty feet. It's a good thing I keep in condition. How did you find the real way in when I couldn't?"

Jay answered with a note of pride in his voice, "A Ute told us. It's our cave."

"You can have the cave, boy. But the gold belongs to me. One of my kinfolk rode with Kid Ruby, and my family's been looking for the gang's loot for over a hundred years. So I've got a right to it!"

Mrs. Weber said softly to Paul, "He's out of his head. Be careful. There's no telling what he might do."

Dobbs shouted at her, "Shut up!" But his eyes were on Jay. "You're so proud of your old-time Utes. Well, how do you think Kid Ruby knew about this cave when other white men didn't? A *Ute* told him—that's how he found out. Frank Hart had a Ute wife at one time. She probably told him about the cave and how to get inside it. Hart dumped her for a white woman, the one who had the baby boy—your precious Bronco Billy Smart. Smart—*ha!* He was

143

never smart enough to think there was secret ink on that old letter of his. He must have known who his father was, though, and didn't want to use his name. He was that smart, anyhow. The Utes must have hated Kid Ruby's using their cave as much as his deserting one of their women for a white one. I'm surprised that any Ute today recalls this cave."

Jay cried, "Outlaws using it to hide stolen money and killing people in it made the cave dirty to my people. They probably didn't want to remember it!"

Dobbs laughed. "Kid Ruby was smart to use this cave. He wasn't afraid of the Indians. He knew no Ute would tell about this place because it had been sacred, and they wouldn't want even more white men knowing about it, especially the army. Maybe they wanted a secret place to hide in themselves when they were fighting the soldiers. They wanted to keep this their secret even after evil white men had defiled it. Kid Ruby thought he had it made when he learned about this cave. Well, now *I've* got it made. I've got his loot."

Mrs. Weber surprised Paul by speaking out in her firmest tone. "Peter, that payroll is not yours. It belongs to the descendants of the men who worked the mines at Fairplay. For that matter, Billy Smart had more right to it than any Dobbs, even if it is stolen money."

"Be quiet, old woman!" Dobbs's voice had risen to a roar. "It belongs to *me*. Bronco Billy Smart may have been

144

a famous man, but he was too stupid to find the secret writing and get rich. And so were all of you when you had that old letter. It took me, nutty Peter Dobbs, to find it."

Jay replied angrily, "I think you are crazy, mister."

"Crazy, huh?" Dobbs patted the canvas sack. "Crazy rich, that's more like it! What do you think gold that was worth forty thousand dollars in 1873 is worth today?" Not waiting for an answer, he chuckled. "Well," he continued, "we had a nice talk, but it's time for me to leave. Oh, just a minute. I almost forgot."

Paul watched the man open the pocket of his jumpsuit and take something from it. It was the ruby-studded buckle. Dobbs said, "Here's your junk jewelry. Keep it for all the good it'll do you. I'm leaving now, but you aren't."

Hearing this, Mrs. Weber gasped. Dobbs turned to her with a smile. "Oh, don't worry, Mrs. Weber. I'm not going to shoot or harm you. I'm not even going to waste my time tying you up again. But I am going to remind you all that I do have a gun, and that it's loaded. So don't try to follow me. I *will* use it if I really have to. I'll find the way you got in. You undoubtedly left it open. Nice of you. Well, I'll be polite. I'll close it for you when I leave!"

"Close it?" cried Mrs. Weber, scrambling to her feet. "You'll be killing us!"

By now Dobbs was at the tunnel entrance. In another moment he had entered it and was out of sight.

Terrible fear gripped Paul Braun as his grandmother's

words struck home. Yes, they knew where to push on the rock to get inside the cavern, but they didn't know how to get out once the entrance had been shut.

Paul asked Jay quickly, "Did the Old One tell you where to push to get out of here?"

"No." Jay's voice sounded deflated. "I could have asked her, but I didn't think of it."

"What're we going to do?" asked Mrs. Weber in a strangled voice.

"*I know!*" Paul replied suddenly. "Jay and I are going to follow Dobbs and jump him before he gets away. Even though he's got a head start, that big bag of gold must be slowing him down. We can catch up to him before he reaches the dancing rock. Are you game, Jay?"

"You bet, Paul. I'll jump him and you hit him on the head with your flashlight hard as you can."

"*No!*" came from a horrified Sally Weber.

"We've got to try, Grandma. It's the only chance we have of getting out of here. Don't worry. We've both got sports shoes with rubber soles on. Dobbs won't hear Jay and me coming. We'll track him like Indians."

"Like the old Utes," Jay told her.

To make sure Dobbs wouldn't see them, Paul and Jay switched off their flashlights the instant they entered the tunnel. Paul went first, groping his way forward in the blackness, moving his feet cautiously so they would make no noise that Dobbs might hear. He wondered if Jay's heart raced the way his did. His was pounding so hard that he was sure the man somewhere ahead of them would hear it.

It seemed to take forever, but finally Paul neared the end of the narrow tunnel. He straightened up and halted to look ahead. *Hurray!* They were in time—the bobbing yellow glow of Pete Dobbs's flashlight was in front of him.

Stepping to the left so Jay could come abreast of him, Paul suddenly felt something brush his left shoulder. His teeth clenched, Paul felt about with one hand. To his great relief his fingers touched the hanging end of a piece of rope. Of course! The rope Dobbs had used to come down from the top of the cave. Paul had not noticed it before when he, Jay, and his grandmother had first entered the narrow tunnel; their flashlights had been beamed directly ahead. And obviously Dobbs had forgotten all about it when he passed by just a few seconds before, probably because he was preoccupied with his own thoughts of getting out and away with all that gold.

"Jay?" hissed Paul.

"I'm here. I'm with you."

"I found Dobbs's rope just now."

"Good. We can tie him up with it once we get him. Come on. I'll lead the way now. Remember, I'll tackle him."

Paul and Jay were about to move forward into the large cavern when suddenly they heard the bark of a pistol shot!

Paul fell to the ground, but no bullet whizzed past to

147

strike the rock behind him. Holding his breath, he became aware of Jay lying next to him. Paul listened and heard other sounds now—shouts and curses, labored breathing, and finally a deep moaning sound as someone fell heavily to the ground.

Paul whispered, "Jay, what is it?"

"I dunno. Be quiet and listen. It's Dobbs—and somebody else."

"Who could that be?"

"*Listen,* I tell you."

Paul strained his ears but now heard only gasps from the cave ahead. Then, all at once, he saw a circle of light. Someone was coming toward them with a flashlight.

Dobbs? Terror dampened Paul's face with cold sweat.

11

ANOTHER
SURPRISE!

"Hey?" came a deep male voice. "Jay, Jay Jenkins, are you in here?"

Paul held his breath but heard Jay getting up.

"Lewis, is that you?" cried the Indian boy.

"Yes, it's me. Sure."

"Lewis, we're over here, Paul and I." Jay switched on his flashlight as Paul got up shakily to his feet.

Now came the sound of running steps and almost immediately the man was beside them. Paul noticed that there was blood on his face. Hurriedly he told the Ute, "Pete Dobbs attacked us in here. He tried to kill us and Grandma. Did you see him? He was on his way out of the cave."

"You bet I did. He shot at me and missed—then I fought

with him and knocked him cold in the tunnel near the cave opening. He doesn't know karate at all. This is his flashlight. So his name is Dobbs, huh?"

Jay took over the explanation. "Yes, he'd been looking for the sacred cave, too, and found it just before we did. To prevent us from telling the police on him, he was going to shut the opening on us and leave us here to die. We don't know the secret of getting out again."

"Don't worry. I left it open. Where is your grandmother, Paul?"

"In another part of this cave. Are you sure Dobbs won't get away?" Then Paul volunteered, "I know where we can get some rope to tie him up. Dobbs used it to get down from the top of the cave and left it dangling. He was in such a hurry to leave that he forgot it. You could go up a ways and cut it off with a knife, then use it to tie him up."

"That's good thinking. He might come to."

Jay told the other Ute, "He has the stagecoach robbery loot with him."

"Is that what it was I hit? I felt something hard at one point when I fought with Dobbs in the dark. It slowed him down."

"What about his gun?" asked Paul.

Scarfe opened his light jacket wide to show it stuffed into the waistband of his trousers. "Now the rope," he said. "I'll cut some off with my pocket knife. Paul, you go get your grandmother."

"Sure."

With the flashlight's beam to guide him, it took only minutes for Paul to go through the tunnel to the petroglyph room for Mrs. Weber. Just before he reached the end he called ahead, "Don't be scared. It's me, Paul. Grandma, it's all right now. A friend of Jay's came and knocked Dobbs out before he left the cave."

"Oh, Paul! Paul!" Mrs. Weber rushed forward, flung herself on him, and held tight. "I've kept praying for you and Jay. Let's get out of here. I want to see the sun more than anything in the whole world."

When the two of them reached the entrance to the cavern they found Lewis Scarfe cutting up lengths of rope to bind Dobbs. As he finished he said, "It won't take long to tie him up. I'll be back in a few minutes. I want to have a good look at this famous cave of my people."

Paul asked, "How did you know we were here?"

Lewis smiled at the question. "When I've tended to our sleeping beauty, Dobbs, I'll come back and tell you. But first things first. On second thought, you come with me, Jay."

Marveling at the man's coolness, Paul stood with his arm comfortingly about his grandmother's shoulder. He was impatient for Lewis to return because he had a lot of questions for him.

When Lewis and Jay re-entered the cavern, Lewis said, "Jay introduced me to your Mr. Dobbs. He says he's a watch repairer at the mall. I never set eyes on him until this afternoon."

Sally Weber told Lewis, "I've known Peter since he was little. He was a nice boy. My son had him over a couple of times, as I recall. He must have gone mad, I think, to have done something like this." She shook her head. "I don't know you, though, Mr. . . . ?"

"Lewis Scarfe's my name. I go to college in the Springs. Like Jay, I'm a Ute. I have a special interest in this cave because of that. Now let's see that stagecoach Jay's been telling me about."

Obediently the two boys flashed their beams about until they focused on the deserted coach.

Scarfe walked about it in respectful silence. Then he asked, "Where are the passengers?"

"We found 'em," volunteered Jay, and he took Lewis to the spot where the skeletons lay. The two of them soon returned.

Scarfe told Paul and Mrs. Weber flatly, "I don't think this is the work of the Utes. They probably had some rifles, but I don't believe they shot these people."

"Then it must have been Kid Ruby," came from Paul.

Jay put in, " 'Red boy,' the Old One called him."

Lewis grunted softly. "Yes, that's what she said—'red' could mean 'ruby' and 'boy,' 'kid.' 'Bus' means 'stage-coach.' " He looked at Paul and his grandmother. "It's because of the Old One that I came out here this afternoon. I couldn't sleep last night for thinking of what I had heard her say. She gets up early, like most very old people, so I went to see her this morning and I talked to her some more in Ute. She was more alert today than the last time I saw her. I got more from her because I had decided beforehand just what to ask. She told me about the petroglyphs outside and the dead tree on top of the cliff. The woman who looks in on the Old One came in while I was there and told me, Jay, that your mother had told her where you and some friends were going. I figured you meant to explore out here, too, on the strength of what the Old One had told you. So I decided to cut a class and drive out myself. Well, I saw two parked cars and when I saw that the driver's registration card in the green one read Mrs. Sally Weber, I knew it was Paul's grandmother. The other car didn't mean anything to me at all. I scouted the ravines, looking for the dead tree. When I found it, it didn't take me long to find the balancing rock."

"Thank God you did!" breathed Mrs. Weber.

Lewis continued, "So I came inside and the first thing I met was your friend Dobbs on his way outside. I hadn't expected him." The Ute smiled. "He hadn't expected me either. I scared him, but he recovered fast enough and started fighting. . . . Well, so far I've seen Dobbs and his rope and the stagecoach and some skeletons. Is there more?"

The two boys looked at each other, and Jay said, "Lewis, you haven't seen the most important part of the cave. We've got to show you the cavern with the rock carvings on the walls."

"More petroglyphs, huh? Lead the way."

Sally Weber protested now, "No. Shouldn't we get Dobbs into the hands of the police first? He has my car keys, too. I want them."

"Don't worry about him, ma'am. He won't get loose."

"We got loose after he tied us up," boasted Paul, and under Scarfe's admiring gaze, he felt a glow of warm pleasure.

"So you were tied up? Where did this happen?"

"Outside the cave, Lewis," explained Jay.

Scarfe said, "So, Dobbs's ropes couldn't hold you, huh? Well, Mrs. Weber, once the word gets about that this old cavern has been rediscovered after so many years—not to mention finding the missing stagecoach, its passengers, and the gold—this cave will be so full of police and reporters and Indian experts that we'd never get to explore it in peace. Two modern-day Utes ought to have the right to see what's in here first, shouldn't we? After all, it once belonged to us."

"It sure did," Jay put in. "I bet the medicine men had their ceremonies in the cavern with the rock carvings."

"More than likely—before the white outlaws took it over."

Jay explained, "Dobbs said a Ute woman told Kid Ruby about it. She was his wife."

Scarfe nodded. "That could be. If she had, it was a bad thing for her to do. Now, let's look at the rest of this place before the local news comes out with the story. It'll be a real sensation." He chuckled, and it was a strange sound in the

154

eerie, echoing cavern. Then he added, "There's something else I'll be looking for in here."

"What?" asked Paul.

"If I find it, I'll tell you. Come on, let's go. Show me the rock carvings."

Paul led the way and the others followed, making their way into the smaller cavern. He stood aside and watched Scarfe's face as the man examined the wall, illuminated by all three flashlights.

The Ute said finally, "Oh, yes, this is where our old medicine men used to come to make magic. Just think, Jay, we're the first of our people to stand here in over a century."

"I know that, Lewis."

"Does the cavern end here?"

Paul replied to the question. "We don't know. This is where we ran into Dobbs. It's as far as we've gone. There isn't anything in the trunks here."

"I noticed that, too, Paul. Let's go down that tunnel over to the left and see where it ends."

The three of them followed Lewis, walking stooped over for some distance. The tunnel led into an even smaller cave, which was strewn with rocks. It ended in a sheer wall. Clearly, this was the end of the cave.

There were no rock carvings here. There didn't seem to be anything at all. But then, just as they turned to leave, Paul spotted the glint of something that winked yellowish at him from between two boulders. What could it be?

155

"Hey, there's something over here," he sang out, going toward the rocks.

When he looked down at it, Paul Braun caught his breath in stunned amazement. What had caught his eye was the gleam of a gold belt buckle worn by a heap of human bones and rags. The buckle was studded with red stones in the shape of a heart—the mate of the one in his shirt pocket.

"*I've found Kid Ruby!*" he called to the others.

Mrs. Weber muttered, "He never left the Territory. He never left the cave! Look, there are other skeletons here, too."

Lewis peered over Paul's shoulder. Then he knelt and played Dobbs's flashlight over the bones. Laughing grimly, he said, "There's an arrow in the chest of every man."

"Ute work?" asked Paul.

"Yes, this would be the old Ute way."

Mrs. Weber exclaimed, "Good heavens, that makes eleven bodies in here."

Jay asked, "Is this what you were looking for, Lewis?"

"No, but I'm not surprised. It adds a big piece to the old puzzle. I think I can tell you what happened here in 1873. Isn't that the year you said the coach disappeared, Jay?"

"Yes, what happened?"

"I'd say that Kid Ruby and his gang waylaid the stage and brought it and the people on it in here. It would have been easy. After all, there weren't any turnoff roads to other towns, and the cave is along the stagecoach's route.

Then he shot the passengers. I think some Utes must have been watching from the top of the cliffs. After a while they followed the coach and the outlaws inside, and probably executed all four of the gang on the spot."

Jay added excitedly, "They didn't dare tell what had happened. So they shut up the old cave and that was that! The army would have hung the Utes if they'd found out what Indians had done to white men, even if they were outlaws."

"That's right, Jay," came from Scarfe. "The old Utes were smart. They gave up the cave as a sacred place because too much devilry had gone on inside it. There were too many dead men here. Kid Ruby may have planned to leave the Territory right after this robbery, but the Utes put an end to that dream. Look here, beside the skeletons. There are pine-knot torches. The Indians must have used them to light their way in here. They probably took Kid Ruby's lanterns away with them, as well as any weapons the outlaws had."

Paul was still looking at Kid Ruby, figuring by the length of his arms and legs that he had been very tall. His grandmother broke in on his thoughts by saying, "Paul, can you get the buckle for me, please?"

Kneeling, the boy pulled the buckle easily from the rotting leather of the old belt and took it over to his grandmother. She in turn presented it to Jay, saying, "You deserve this, Jay. You keep one of these and Paul will keep the other. I doubt that you'll ever want to wear it after this,

157

but you keep it as a memento of a real old western adventure. In a way this one is a family heirloom, too, so I can give it where I choose."

"Thank you, *wano momets.*" Jay's thanks were simple and dignified as he put the buckle into his shirt pocket.

Paul looked on, pleased with his grandmother's gesture. She said, slowly now, "I wonder how Great Aunt Sophronia found out that the Frank Hart she fell in love with and married was the notorious Kid Ruby? I'll bet she didn't know at first. When she did find out, it must have been a terrible discovery for her. She must have learned this just before their son, Billy, was born. Her family probably knew, too, and somebody wisely removed Hart's name from the Bible to protect her and her son. I imagine Sophronia told Billy who his father was when he was old enough to know, and it probably was she who chose the name Smart for him to use. Like everyone else in the Territory, she never knew what happened to Frank Hart. After seven years her missing husband was considered legally dead and she was free to marry again. Her new husband's name, John Blake, was written over Hart's in the Bible. Poor little Billy. Now we can see why he never wore the buckle his father sent him. What a secret to carry all his life!"

Now she turned to Lewis to ask, "Mr. Scarfe, what will happen to the gold?"

"I don't really know. That kind of thing isn't in my line. In 1873 it was worth forty thousand dollars, but with today's gold prices it will be worth far, far more. State authorities will probably take it while they investigate all these old deaths. They'll bury the people. If the company that shipped the gold is still around doing business, it might be able to claim it. Some of it could even belong to this Dobbs guy in the long run, since he was the first one inside here—wasn't he?"

"Yes," replied Mrs. Weber.

Lewis shrugged. "But on the other hand he's guilty of attempting to murder you three and assaulting me." Scarfe blew out his breath. "That alone ought to add up to enough to put him in prison for a long time. He won't be enjoying his loot even if he gets it. You know, this is going to turn out to be a big mess for the county and state people for a time. But one good thing has come out of it besides the discovery of the gold and the old coach."

Paul asked, "What's that?"

"Colorado history has been set straight on something important. This proves that the Utes didn't attack the coach. If they had, they would have killed the passengers with arrows, like they did to kill the outlaws. The Utes got to the gang before the army and the U.S. marshals did, and they hung onto their secret so they wouldn't have to do any explaining to white men, who probably wouldn't have listened sympathetically to them anyway. As Jay said, they would have hanged our people. Of course, the army didn't find any evidence of the coach in the Ute camps when they came to search them." He chuckled. "It must have tickled them—to leave the coach in here, as well as Kid Ruby and his men, who had defiled their cave. They didn't want the stagecoach gold. They wanted revenge on Kid Ruby, and they got it. And they got something else into the bargain, too."

"What?" asked Paul.

"Think about the old coach and ask yourself if something is missing there?"

Paul made a mental picture of it standing forlorn with its shafts down on the cave floor. Suddenly he knew what Scarfe meant. He shouted out, "Horses! There weren't any horse skeletons!"

"That's right. Not a one. The Utes took all the horses away with them when they left the cave. No Ute would leave a horse to starve to death. They loved horses. They didn't have any use for gold, but for good horses they sure did. Horses and mules said wealth to them. They were very skilled at blotting out white men's brands, so no searcher would ever have spotted any animal that had belonged to anyone inside here."

"Horses?" mused Jay. "I should have thought of that, too."

"Well, this isn't exactly a horse society today. Our ancestors will forgive you, Jay."

Paul now turned to Jay. "You've sure got a neat ending to your essay. But I still have a problem. Should I end mine by revealing that Bronco Billy Smart's real father was an outlaw and a killer? What do you say, Grandma?"

For a moment Mrs. Weber pondered. Then she said,

"Go on, tell it. It can't hurt Billy now, and I think it's very interesting. An outlaw will do very nicely in our family tree if we can't have a pirate. Kid Ruby is history. Write about him."

Paul stood silent for a moment, then said, "All right." Wow, what he had learned, all in one day! With the help of four Coloradans, three of them Indians, he, an easterner, had cleared up a mystery—and solved a crime that had happened over a hundred and ten years before. What would the rest of the summer be like after starting out so well?

Lewis Scarfe broke his train of thought by asking, "From what I gather, you two boys were going to attack a gun-toting man all by yourselves."

Mrs. Weber chimed in, "They surely were. I couldn't stop them."

By the light of his flashlight, Paul could see that the Ute man was grinning broadly. "That was pretty brave of you," he said.

Jay smiled back. "You don't know what we call ourselves, do you—a Delaware brave and Ute brave."

"Well, you've earned the right to call yourselves that."

As they headed out of the cavern shortly afterward, Mrs. Weber told Scarfe, "We're all in your debt. We won't forget that."

Lewis seemed embarrassed now. Then, staring at the coach he told them all, "And our ancestors owe you all something, too, something that's been a long time coming—justice. Come on, let's drag Mr. Dobbs outside the

161

cave. I'll guard him and the gold while you get your car keys from him and drive off to notify the first patrolman you meet."

Suddenly Paul turned to Jay to ask, "Hey, are you as hungry as I am? We never got to our picnic lunch."

"You bet I am."

Mrs. Weber smiled at both boys. "You can eat while I drive. Come on, my braves!"

AUTHOR'S NOTE

While visiting schools during the last few years I have repeatedly been asked by young students to write them a mystery story.

In reading the Works Progress Administration Writers' Program book, *Colorado: A Guide to the Highest State,* originally published in 1941, I ran across one sentence that gave me the genesis of my mystery. It is on page 230 and reads:

> In 1873 a four-horse stage carrying five passengers and $40,000 in gold is said to have entered the pass and to have disappeared without a trace.

(The reference here is to Ute Pass, the route between Colorado Springs and the mining camp of Fairplay.)

163

I do not know what became of the actual coach, its passengers, or the gold. Except for the material about the Ute Indians and Buffalo Bill Cody and his Wild West Show, my book is fiction.

I am indebted to Mary M. Davis of the Pike's Peak Library District, Colorado Springs, Colorado, for graciously sending me material on old-time outlaws. I also owe a debt to Josephine Horton of the Shamrock Rock Shop, Riverside, California, for facts about old rubies, antique jewelry, and their value. In addition I must thank Julie Rich of the Riverside Public Library, Riverside, California, who told me how summer reading games operate these days, long after I ceased working as a children's librarian.

Finally, two very remarkable children I met while visiting at Ramona-Alessandro School, San Bernardino, California, are involved with this book, having discussed it with me. They are Utes, and I hope that when they read my mystery they will be pleased to see their native language used and will remember me.

PATRICIA BEATTY
JANUARY 1985

About the Author

A long-time resident of Southern California, Patricia Beatty was born in Portland, Oregon. She was graduated from Reed College there, and then taught high-school English and history for four years. Later she held various positions as science and technical librarian and also as a children's librarian. She has taught Writing Fiction for Children at several branches of the University of California.

She has had a number of historical novels published by Morrow, several of them dealing with the American West in the 1860 to 1895 period. They include such widely acclaimed titles as *Wait for Me, Watch for Me, Eula Bee; Melinda Takes a Hand;* and *Eight Mules from Monterey,* which is a Notable Children's Trade Book in the Field of Social Studies. Another of her Notable Children's Trade Books, *Lupita Mañana,* was also chosen as a Jane Addams Children's Book Award honor book.

Pat Beatty is married to a professor of economics at the University of California, Riverside, and has a married daughter, Alexandra Beatty Stewart.